★ American Girl®

Luciana

Braving the Deep

BY ERIN TEAGAN

Scholastic Inc.

Published by Scholastic Inc., *Publishers since 1920.* SCHOLASTIC and associated logos are trademarks and/or registered trademarks of Scholastic Inc. The publisher does not have any control over and does not assume any responsibility for author or third-party websites or their content.

This book is a work of fiction. Names, characters, places, and incidents are either the product of the author's imagination or are used fictitiously, and any resemblance to actual persons, living or dead, business establishments, events, or locales is entirely coincidental.

Book design by Suzanne LaGasa
Author photo by Patty Schuchman
Cover and interior illustrations by Lucy Truman

americangirl.com/service

ISBN 978-1-338-18650-5

10 9 8 7 6 5 4 3 2 1   18 19 20 21 22

Printed in the U.S.A.   23 • First printing 2018

FOR MEREDITH, MIKAELA,
SOFIA, AND MOLLY

CONTENTS

CHAPTER 1

GOOD-BYES

My best friend, Raelyn, and I sat on my front lawn under a mulberry tree. It was August in Virginia, which meant it was as hot as the surface of Venus outside. At least, that's what it felt like. We were watching my little sister, Isadora, play with her wagon, filling it with pinecones and dandelions while Mom and Dad packed up the car. We were also supposed to be saying good-bye. In just fifteen minutes, I would be on my way to a two-week youth astronaut training camp.

"So, you're sure this camp is safe for kids?" Raelyn asked, picking at the grass in front of her.

"Yep." I smiled at her. "I'm sure."

Raelyn laid back in the grass. "At least promise me you'll be careful."

"Okay, *Mom*," I joked, and she threw some grass at me.

"I'm just saying this camp sounds like serious business," Raelyn explained.

I felt a streak of excitement go up my spine. After I went to Space Camp over spring break, I wanted more. Sure, I had my ups and downs being away from home for the first time, but the experience was awesome. So, as soon as I heard about this training program from my friend Ella from Space Camp, I knew that I had to go. Ella and I applied to the program and in the end, only six kids from across the country were accepted. I was so proud—and okay, a little bit nervous.

"You're right," I told Raelyn. "It is kind of serious. Anyway, art camp isn't always completely safe either."

Raelyn gave me a questioning look. She'd be going to the art camp down the street at the rec center, a camp we normally did together.

I put on a serious face. "You know, all those pointy paintbrushes and sharp drawing pencils, not to mention the highly flammable kiln in the back room."

Raelyn laughed, sitting up. "Yeah, I'll try not to run with scissors."

I knew Raelyn was just trying to make me smile, but I would miss her. A lot.

"Did you pack your flippers?" Raelyn asked.

"Do you mean my fins?" I said with a laugh. "No, I don't even have any. Besides, they will give us all the equipment there." Our mission at camp would be to dive to Cetus, an underwater habitat where real astronauts train for life in space. We'd live there for twenty-four hours, perform experiments, and practice space walks on the ocean floor. Going to Cetus would take me one step closer to being an astronaut and my dream of being the first girl on Mars.

Just then, Isadora came barreling over, a dandelion in her hand. "*Flor!*" she said, using the Spanish word for "flower." My parents had adopted her two months ago from an orphanage in Chile, the country where my family was from. I had wanted a baby sister my whole life and I still couldn't believe she was here.

I took the dandelion from her and pretended to gobble it up, smacking my lips. She giggled and ran off to her yellow plastic car by the front walk. Dad was just coming out of the garage with a diaper bag, Mom close behind with Isadora's stuffed penguin and a handful of toys. My bag was already in the trunk.

"By the way," I said to Raelyn, "my parents scheduled Izzy's surgery." My heart throbbed with worry.

Adoptions usually took a long time but we were able to bring Isadora home so fast because she had a heart defect and needed treatment. Not to mention surgery.

Raelyn looked up. "When is it?"

"It's a few days after I get back from camp," I said.

Raelyn shimmied closer to me in the grass. "Try not to worry about it while you're at camp, okay? You've been excited about this program all summer."

We were quiet for a second, watching my little sister try to ride her car over one of the garden beds. It was hard to get the surgery out of my head. She was so little. The thought of her—

"Seriously, are you thinking about it now? Stop," Raelyn said.

"I'm not thinking about anything." But I had pulled every petal off my dandelion without even realizing it.

"Seriously. Don't ruin your time at camp. Izzy will be fine while you're gone," Raelyn said.

I sighed. "I know. Thanks, Rae. What am I going to do without you and your advice when I'm away?"

Raelyn took hold of my hand. We flopped back in the grass and lay in the shade of the tree, twirling the purple stripes in our hair. We had each dyed one little section of our hair to match. A friendship stripe.

"Five minutes!" Dad called from the driveway.

"Lulululu!" Isadora called. She pedaled in our direction and parked her yellow plastic car next to us. "Lulu." She opened the door and patted the seat.

Raelyn laughed. "Aw, she wants you to get in."

Isadora bounced.

I draped one of my legs over the door of the car. "Lulu is too big!" I said to Isadora, but she wasn't convinced. She got out of the car and pulled my arm.

"Come on, big sister," Raelyn said. "Get yourself in there."

I folded myself into the car, backing butt-first through the toddler-sized doorway, my head hitting the yellow plastic roof. Isadora clapped.

"One of your legs is still out!" Raelyn said, snorting with laughter as if this was the most hysterical thing she'd ever seen.

I pulled my other leg in close to my chest and wedged it inside the toy car, giving Raelyn a look. "Your turn next," I threatened.

But Raelyn was laughing so hard, I couldn't help

laughing too, which was difficult to do while jammed inside a toy car.

Isadora stopped clapping and tried to climb in with me, getting mad when I couldn't make room. "Lulu's too big," I told her. Then, somehow, she managed to tip the car over—with me still inside.

I face-planted into the grass, my arms and legs too packed into the car to catch myself. "Rae!" I called, my words muffled in the ground. I was trapped in the yellow plastic car. "Raelyn-this-isn't-funny-help-me."

I pushed against the car, my head hitting the top and my knees locked against the steering wheel. I didn't like this game anymore. What if I was really stuck? Like, so stuck nobody could even help me? I felt a flash of panic. My heart thumped in my ears, beating too fast, and all of a sudden I couldn't catch my breath. I pushed my knees against the steering wheel harder. "RAELY—"

"Can I help you?" She grinned, lifting the car up enough to dump me out onto the lawn.

I took deep breaths, sprawled on the grass, Raelyn next to me still laughing her head off, the sun bright in our faces. "Seriously, you okay?" she asked, catching her breath.

"Yep," I said, thankful she couldn't hear that my heart was still racing.

Sometimes my heart just leapt into panic mode. Like that time Raelyn and I rearranged her room during a sleepover and I got wedged between the wall and her bed or when I accidentally locked myself in the girls' locker room at school. But I could always count on Raelyn when I needed a rescue.

Isadora toddled over and squeezed into the little space between us, putting her head on my shoulder and her feet in Raelyn's face. It wasn't long before she was sleeping.

"Time to go!" Dad called.

Raelyn helped me carry a droopy Isadora over to the car. Who knew a toddler could be so heavy?

"Oh dear, is Izzy sleeping?" Mom flitted around her, feeling her forehead and taking her pulse to check for any changes.

"Mom?" I said, feeling a spike of nerves.

"She's okay. Pulse is fine." She kissed Isadora's rosy cheek. "I just worry when she sleeps so soon after waking up from her morning nap, you know?"

Sleepiness. Weak pulse. Those were the symptoms of my little sister's heart condition. "Just two more weeks," I said. "And then she'll be all better. We won't have to worry anymore."

Mom gently tugged my hair. "A mother always worries." She took Isadora, who was snoring little baby snores. "I'll get her into her car seat," she said, leaving Raelyn and me alone.

Raelyn and I hated saying good-bye. It took us almost an hour to say good-bye when she went to Colorado one summer for three weeks for her uncle's wedding, and even longer when I left for an entire Christmas break in first grade to visit Abuelita in Chile. But Mom and Dad and Isadora were already in the car waiting for me.

"I'll bring you back a shell from the bottom of the ocean, okay?" I said.

"And I'll make pinch pots for us in the highly flammable kiln." She smiled.

Then we did our secret handshake from second grade and hugged each other until Dad tooted the horn.

CHAPTER 2

WELCOME TO CAMP

The training program was a two-hour drive to the coast. It shared a small peninsula of land with a space flight facility, with the bay on one side and the ocean on the other. I cracked the window as we got closer, the steamy salt air floating into the car.

Isadora still slept, even when we turned off the main road of shopping centers and big stores full of beach stuff and headed toward the bay. The road narrowed and we passed a sign for the space flight facility with a rocket pointed to a starry night sky. And then we passed a banner for the youth training program, and I got so excited I could barely stay in my seat belt.

"I'll stay here with Izzy. You go with Dad to get checked in," Mom said.

"Dad," I said, looking around as we got out of the car, "it's beautiful." There was a large grassy area with a giant airplane hangar and a dozen or so yellow cottages at the water's edge. The cottages were stuck right in the sand, the bay calm and blue green behind them. It looked like a resort, not a youth astronaut training camp, even with all the kids walking around.

"Luciana!" It was Ella, running out of the hangar. I dodged a group of kids lugging their duffel bags across the grassy area and raced to meet her. We'd been sending postcards back and forth for the past few months, but I hadn't seen her since we left Space Camp.

"Ella!" She looked nearly the same—brown hair pulled back in a ponytail and greenish-hazel eyes— except with more freckles across her nose, probably from the summer sun.

"Hurry and go check in," Ella urged. "I can't wait to show you our cottage!"

I grabbed Dad and pulled him toward the hangar where there was a giant "REGISTER HERE" sign. Inside the hangar, equipment and workstations filled an open space wide enough for the biggest planes. As I took in the enormous room, from its cool concrete floors to the stories-high ceiling, the entire place echoed with the voices of kids and families. There was a greenhouse in the middle of the hangar; a computer station with monitors climbing up the wall; something that looked like an engine, all falling apart on a table; machines big and small everywhere; and a cylinder as tall and wide as a house in the corner of the room. I was pretty sure that was the underwater astronaut training pool.

Dad squeezed my hand and we followed a mom and kid toward the front of the hangar with a wall of windows looking out to the bay. Registration was on a long table with three signs. "AVIATION." "ROCKET SCIENCE." "CETUS."

I marched us over to the "CETUS" sign where a woman holding a clipboard stood up. Her name tag said "Sarah."

"I'm Luciana Vega," I said, waving.

"It's so nice to meet you." She made a check next to my name and shook our hands. "I'm Sarah, one of your Cetus counselors. Here's the key to your cottage, a map of the camp, and your name badge." She tapped her clipboard. "We're just waiting for one more person and then we'll beach-buggy over to the ocean side together for a welcome bonfire on the beach."

I was going to ride in a beach buggy! For a welcome bonfire! I clapped. I couldn't help it.

Sarah laughed. "Go ahead and unpack and get settled. I'll see you in a little bit."

When we got back outside, Mom waved to us from the beach.

Isadora was awake, pressing her little toes deep into the pale sand and when I sat next to her, she plopped into my lap. I hugged her and kissed her cheeks. Suddenly, sitting here with my new baby sister made beach buggies and yellow cottages in the sand feel not so exciting.

"I'm going to miss Izzy so much," I said.

"This program is an amazing opportunity for you," Mom said. "You'll have a wonderful time."

I nodded. The underwater habitat was normally reserved for training real astronauts who were preparing to go to space. The youth training program had special permission to use the underwater habitat so kids could feel what it was like to be an actual astronaut. It *was* an amazing opportunity for someone like me.

"Want us to help you unpack?" Dad asked as Mom stood up and dusted the sand off her legs.

I shook my head. "It's okay." The sun was starting to get low in the sky. I knew they had a long drive back. I took a breath. "I've got it."

"Don't forget, you can call us anytime," Mom said. We hugged, and then I watched my family as they walked to the parking lot, Isadora laying her head on Dad's shoulder. For a minute, watching them leave, I felt overwhelmed with homesickness, but then Ella burst out of one of the cottages and ran to me. "I saved you a bottom bunk. Come on!"

I jogged along the sand with her to the first cottage, squinting past the bright yellow paint to read the sign over the door: "Chincoteague." Inside there were two sets of bunk beds pushed against the wall, a bathroom, and a dresser for all of our clothes.

Ella patted a bottom bunk. "Take this one so we can be next to each other." She had already claimed the other one, her stars and moon bedding neatly laid out.

But just as I was about to throw my sheets onto the bed, we heard a helicopter. The whirring sound got closer and closer until it seemed as though the helicopter was right overhead. We bounced up and looked out the window. Kids were gathering around the grassy area where I saw a helicopter pad.

"I think it's landing here!" I said.

"Does that say Mars Extreme?" Ella asked, her mouth open.

"Mars what?" I asked.

"It does. It says Mars Extreme!" Ella hopped up

and down, something I'd never seen Ella do before. The Ella I knew from Space Camp was serious. And definitely not prone to overexcitement.

"Are you feeling okay?" I asked, laughing.

"You don't know Mars Extreme?" Ella said. "The company owned by Lance Jacobs? The famous space inventor?"

"Oh!" I said. Suddenly, I knew who she was talking about: the guy I'd seen on TV with all of his fancy electric cars and on the cover of a science magazine wearing a space suit. He was the guy who promised to send the first people to Mars.

"Do you think it's really him?" Ella said.

I tossed my sheets and blanket onto my bed. "Let's find out."

We ran out of the cabin just as the helicopter touched down. Ella grabbed my hand, and we held our breaths, waiting to see who would come out.

CHAPTER 3

MARS EXTREME

We didn't have to wonder long. When the helicopter doors popped open, a man wearing a leather jacket covered with space patches jumped out, ducking low to avoid the rotors. I would have recognized his curly, wild hair anywhere.

Ella made a squealing sound next to me.

"What's Lance Jacobs doing here?" I wondered. Did he work for the training program? Was he looking for a kid to take with him to Mars?

"Good afternoon!" Mr. Jacobs said, striding up to the cluster of kids from all the different camp programs who were crowding on the lawn. "Beautiful day to start your space training!" And it was. Even the heat felt less suffocating by the water with the soft breeze coming from the bay. He shook hands, starting down the line, and when he reached Ella and me wearing our Cetus name badges, he stopped.

"I hope you know what it means to be part of this program," he said. "I've been to Cetus myself many times." I noticed a few other kids with Cetus badges push to the front of the crowd to hear better. "You should feel lucky to be here. You'll be ahead of the rest of your astronaut class when the time comes. Not many kids get the chance to train where real astronauts train." For a second it felt like he was talking only to me.

That's when I noticed the girl standing behind Mr. Jacobs. She was tall with the same thick, wavy hair as his.

"Dad?" she said.

Lance Jacobs had a daughter?

"Are you going to check me in and help me unpack?" she asked.

And she was coming to camp?

Our counselor, Sarah, jogged over. "I've got her, sir. We'll get her all set up."

"She's in the Cetus program!" Ella whispered in my ear, obviously thrilled.

Mr. Jacobs kissed his daughter on the cheek and with a wave, joined the rest of his team on the helicopter. We all watched it take off and glide through the clouds.

The kids from Aviation and Rocket Science dispersed until there were just six of us left on the lawn with Sarah.

"Welcome to the Cetus program," she said, looking around at our now-gathered team. "As Mr. Jacobs mentioned, you are taking part in a unique training program for future astronauts that will give you real training experience.

"This is your crew." Sarah motioned to all of us, six kids lined up like we were reporting for some kind of duty. "You are all highly accomplished for your age and you outshined dozens of kids to earn a place here." She smiled at us. "One of you won the state science fair. One of you spent your summer on a boat in the Arctic. Two of you received the rare and admirable Fail Smart patch at Space Camp this year." I nudged Ella and she winked, and I felt my face heat up. "One of you skipped a few grades and is getting college credit for this camp."

We all looked hard at one another. I knew it wasn't me or Ella. Could it have been Lance Jacob's kid? Was she also a genius?

"One of you was a national swimming champion," Sarah continued, and I was pretty sure it was the kid puffing his chest out. The one with the buzz cut. "By the end of these two weeks, you'll know all of that and more about one another. You kids will be a family.

"Everything we do here is to prepare the team for

our mission to the underwater habitat, Cetus," Sarah explained. "Taking skills tests and practice dives in the pool is part of your mission training. You'll be assigned a partner project where you will build, create, or grow something that will be used on Cetus. All of this preparation and training is for one twenty-four-hour mission."

Another counselor, Marcus, according to his name tag, came out of the hangar with a badge for the new girl.

"Thanks," she said. "I'm Claire Jacobs, by the way," even though we all hadn't had a chance to introduce ourselves yet.

But no one said anything. Claire shifted the bag she still carried and shook our hands, just like her dad did. "That was my dad, Lance Jacobs. I'm sure you already figured that out." She made a goofy smile, whispering the last part like it was a big secret. "Anyway, um," she said, turning to Sarah, "where should I put my bag?"

"Oh! Right. Let's get you moved in. You're in the Chincoteague cabin with Ella and Luciana."

I swear Ella stopped breathing for a minute. I bumped her with my hip because she was being ridiculous. So, Claire had a famous dad, but that didn't just automatically mean she was a super-awesome kid, right?

Sarah and Claire started toward our cabin. "Make

your way to the beach buggies with Marcus. We'll catch up," Sarah called over her shoulder.

We followed Marcus to a sandy driveway next to the hangar.

"Well, I'm Cole, the national swimming champion," the kid with the buzz cut said. "And actually I've won like a thousand swim meets."

Marcus rubbed Cole's head. "Can we call you Buzz?"

"Like Buzz Aldrin, the astronaut?" he asked. "Yes, you can."

"I'm Luciana Vega," I said. "And this is my friend Ella Emerick. We went to Space Camp together."

Ella waved. "I'm not the genius kid, in case you were wondering."

"You must be the Fail Smart team?" another boy named Thomas said, and we nodded, Ella's cheeks turning pink.

"That sounds like a cool award," the third boy on our team added. "I'm Dominic, by the way." He stuck out his hand formally, and I shook it.

With the introductions made, we climbed into the beach buggies, which were heavy-duty golf carts with giant wheels that could drive on sand. As soon as Claire and Sarah were back, we took off for the ocean on the other side of the peninsula, by the space flight facility. We drove across the grounds of the training program, down a sandy road, and through some tall grass, parking right at the ocean dunes.

We peeled out of the buggies, flicked our shoes off, and walked down a path to the beach. It was getting dark, and the sky was pink and purple over the quiet ocean.

"Look—the launch pad," Ella said, pointing down at the beach.

The launch pad at the space flight facility was full of construction vehicles, cranes, diggers, and a bunch of scaffolding.

"My dad launches rockets from here all the time," Claire said, quickening her pace as she moved past us on the path.

"That's so cool," Ella said under her breath.

"Was his the one that exploded?" Buzz called after her, but she was already on the beach, where Sarah and Marcus were digging a pit for the bonfire by the water's edge. "It happened just a few months ago. BOOM!" He ran down the rest of the way.

These were the kinds of things I didn't love to hear about. The explosions. The burning up on reentry.

Emergencies when you were hundreds of miles from Earth and safety. But these were all astronaut realities.

"How did the rocket explode?" I asked, taking a seat next to Ella on a little piece of driftwood.

"There was a problem during takeoff," Marcus explained, stepping back as the bonfire crackled to life. "One of the engines failed and the rocket exploded."

"Rocket stuff is very dangerous and deadly," Buzz said.

"It was an uncrewed launch and there were no injuries," Marcus told us, "but it just goes to show you how risky space flight can be. They've fixed the problem and they're planning for another rocket launch in a few months."

Marcus handed me a stick and we passed around chocolate and graham crackers and marshmallows to make s'mores.

"It's important to remember," Sarah added, "that dreams aren't meant to come easy. Even in failure, there is progress."

I knew what Sarah was saying was true. Getting the Fail Smart award was an honor, even though it was given to us after we had kind of messed up at Space Camp and lost the robot-building challenge. Still, the award recognized that we took risks, even though we knew we might fail, something I was really proud of.

Ella and I put our roasting sticks in the bonfire, each of us with two marshmallows stacked on top of each other for maximum gooey goodness.

Marcus stood up, pointing into the ocean with his marshmallow roasting stick. "Cetus is right out there, thirty feet under the water. Named after the constellation that represents a sea monster," he said, "Cetus is the next best thing to being in outer space if astronauts need to practice their EVAs."

"Extravehicular activities," Ella interrupted as if she couldn't help herself. "Space walks. Sorry."

Marcus took a bite of his marshmallow. "Yes, exactly, thank you," he said with a full mouth. "An EVA is when the astronaut leaves the spacecraft. Outside of Cetus, the astronauts use weight belts so they can walk on the ocean floor. It's kind of like how they'd walk on the moon, in an environment that's similar to reduced gravity. Plus, while they're down there, astronauts can get a taste of what it feels like to be isolated from the rest of the world."

And from their families, I thought with a pang.

"When do we get to go to Cetus?" Ella asked.

"Next Wednesday, but first you'll have three tests to pass: a treading water test, a two-part scuba skills test, and a test dive in the underwater astronaut trainer. We'll announce the teams the night before the mission," Sarah said.

"Aren't we all on the same team? The Cetus team?" I asked.

"Yes, but within the Cetus team, we'll divide into a mission control team and a dive team," Marcus said.

"How will you decide who does what?" Thomas asked.

"Your skills tests will determine which team you are on," Marcus said. "You definitely have to pass all three to be considered for the dive team."

"Well, then I'll definitely be on the dive team," Claire blurted out.

Really? I thought, shooting a look at Ella, who just stared at Claire in awe.

"All of the roles are equally important for the success of the mission," Sarah said.

"But not equally awesome," Buzz complained. "Mission control is so boring."

The marshmallow I was slow-roasting caught on fire. Did Ella know about this? That there was a chance we wouldn't go to Cetus after all? All at once the bonfire felt too hot on my skin. The damp, humid air was suffocating. If I didn't get a spot on the dive team, what was even the point of all this? I blew out my marshmallow.

"Does everyone have to take all the skills tests?" Claire asked, munching on a graham cracker. "Because I've pretty much done all those things my whole life with my dad. You could call him and ask if you want."

I groaned inwardly. This girl and all of her bragging were starting to bother me.

"Everyone has to pass each test," Marcus said. "If you don't pass the first time, you'll get the chance to make it up. Don't worry about teams just yet. By next Wednesday, you might surprise yourself and discover that you'd rather be in mission control than on the dive team. Or vice versa."

Buzz snorted. "Yeah, right. Raise your hand if you want to go to Cetus."

Six hands shot up.

Houston, we had a problem.

CHAPTER 4

TREADING WATER

That night when we got back to the cabin, the first thing I saw was my bedding rolled up on the floor and an unfamiliar fluorescent pink flowered blanket on my bed. I felt my face get hot. Someone moved my stuff? And put it on the floor? I rushed over to save my pillow, which was half touching the dirty tile.

"Oh," Claire said from behind me. "I hope you don't mind. I can't sleep on the top bunk."

I shook out one of my sheets, which was now sandy thanks to her.

"We don't mind," Ella said, and I squinted at her. "I mean, you don't mind, do you, Luci?"

"I guess not—"

Claire gave me a hug. She smelled like spicy flowers. "Thank you." She grabbed her toothbrush and disappeared into the bathroom.

"What?" Ella said, feeling my stink eye. "I'm sorry. I just—"

"She put my bedding on the floor where there's sand and who knows what else!"

"Yeah," she said. "That wasn't nice." But it didn't seem like she really meant it.

I didn't like the way Ella was acting. Just because Claire had a space celebrity dad, it didn't mean that she could do whatever she wanted. And it certainly didn't automatically make her the best at everything. Why couldn't Ella see that?

"What should we do?" Ella asked.

"Forget it." I sighed and threw my sheets up to the top bunk. By the time I made up my new bed, which was very hard to do when you're trying not to fall off the whole time, both Ella and Claire were already in their pajamas and crawling under their own covers.

I heard them talking while I brushed my teeth. About how Claire didn't have any brothers or sisters and how she had a little kitten named Pudding. Ella came from a big family and had to share her room with two sisters who were constantly stealing her things. So, I knew what she was thinking: that Claire had the perfect life. A kitten of her own. No siblings to take her stuff or share her room.

I lay wide awake, up high in the top bunk, thinking about Cetus and skills tests and how not everyone would get to be on the dive team. Even with the air-conditioning blowing from the ceiling, I felt hot and homesick.

I turned my pillow onto the cool side and pictured myself passing all the skills tests and diving to Cetus. I saw myself ahead of my astronaut class in the space program. I imagined sending messages to my parents from Mars. "Life is great up here," I'd say. "I haven't met the locals yet," I'd joke.

I knew I could get on the dive team and I finally fell asleep believing it.

The next morning after breakfast, we put on our bathing suits and met the rest of our crew at the underwater astronaut trainer. It was taller than a two-story house. Deep enough to hold a killer whale. There was a ramp that wound around and up to the top of the twenty-five-foot-deep pool. Ella, Claire, and I walked slowly, peeking into the portholes as we circled around.

"I've never been in a pool like this," I said.

"You haven't?" Claire said, like this was an everyday pool to her.

Ella climbed up the ramp to the next porthole. "Me neither but it doesn't look like a big deal."

"That's a long ladder," I said, joining Ella at her porthole.

Claire shrugged. "I've seen taller."

The ladder went from the top all the way to the deep bottom. There was a giant apparatus made out of pipes on which astronauts-in-training made repairs and replaced equipment. Marcus had explained that this was good practice for astronauts, because performing these activities in the water felt similar to doing them in space. In the middle of all the pipes was a dome with a small door, about the size of our kitchen pantry at home. From what Sarah had told us earlier about the pool, I knew it was a storage closet used during practice EVAs.

Buzz pushed past us on the ramp, the rest of the boys stopping to walk with us. We took our time, inspecting the pool through each porthole.

"Have you ever been in an underwater astronaut trainer before?" I asked the quiet boy named Thomas.

He shook his head and looked through the porthole

again, squinting up to the water's surface. "How many minutes do we have to tread water today?" he asked.

"Fifteen," Ella said.

Claire pushed away from the porthole. "That's it? A lousy fifteen minutes?"

"That seems long enough to me," I said.

"That's what it said in the camp program," Ella said, smoothing down her ponytail. "I think that's a pretty standard water test."

"Yep," I said. "Totally standard." But when I peeked through the porthole again, I felt a squeeze in my chest because I'd never seen water so deep.

When we reached the top, the carpeted ramp widened into a large space with gear hanging on rolling racks and benches set along the railing. I peered over the railing back down to the floor of the hangar where the Aviation kids were taking apart a giant engine. Realizing how far up I was, my stomach did a backflip.

"Is there a shallow end?" I asked.

"What, are you scared?" Buzz said, grinning while hanging his towel on a hook.

"She's not scared of anything," Ella said for me.

And since I saw Claire standing right there beside her, I added, "I can't wait to get in this really deep pool."

"There's a ledge," Sarah said, stepping into the pool next to Marcus. The water only went up to their waists. "See? It extends halfway across the pool. It's only three feet deep."

We gathered around, looking over the edge, and I thought how from up here it seemed like a regular old pool. I got chills and maybe it was from thinking of all the deep water, but also maybe it was from imagining all those real astronauts, standing where I stood, just like me, ready for their first challenge in the underwater astronaut trainer.

"Like we talked about last night," Marcus said, dunking himself in the shallow part of the pool. "You will have to pass three skills tests before you can be considered for the dive team."

My mouth felt dry and I thought about what Lance Jacobs had said. Going to Cetus would put us a step ahead of the rest of the kids in the world who wanted to be astronauts. If I ever wanted to be the first girl on Mars, I *had* to be on the dive team—which made these the most important tests I'd ever have to take.

"Today we'll be treading water. Fifteen minutes. That's our first skills test," Marcus said.

"Swimming goggles are okay, but otherwise you

don't need any equipment, so go ahead and hop on in," Sarah said, waving us into the water.

Ella and I slid into the water together and swam around. I felt more relaxed, looking down with my goggles into the bright blue of the pool. This wasn't so bad. From here I could see the EVA apparatus clearly and I noticed there was a basketball hoop and a few bowling balls at the bottom of the pool.

"Cooooool," Thomas said, swimming next to me. Claire was already treading water in the deep part of the pool, and I heard Sarah tell her to save her strength for the test.

Buzz took a running start and cannonballed into the water, coming up sputtering. "Whoa. That's deep."

"No cannonballs in the underwater astronaut trainer!" said a booming voice from outside of the pool. A guy wearing a bandanna on his head stood over us looking very official and serious. We all stopped splashing around and got serious too. Especially Buzz.

"Hey, Pirate Pete," Sarah said.

And then the Pirate Pete guy broke into a grin, chuckling and putting down the scuba masks in his arms. "What did the ocean say to the pirate?"

"I don't know," Buzz said.

"Nothing! It just waved!" He snorted and clapped at his own joke and Marcus and Sarah groaned.

"Pirate Pete is our scuba expert," Sarah said. "He's in charge of gear and safety and he'll be with us on Cetus as well."

"And today, I'll be your professional timer." He grabbed a handheld stopwatch from the basket on the table and slipped the cord over his head. He held it up, poised to press the start button. "You ready?"

We pulled away from the side, floating out into the open water.

"Ready . . . set . . . go!"

Within the first thirty seconds, I realized just how long treading water for fifteen minutes in the middle of a twenty-five-foot-deep pool was going to feel. My muscles burned. But when I glanced around at the rest of my campmates, nobody else seemed to be struggling. Claire and Buzz were having a conversation about their goggles as if they treaded water like this every day. Ella looked focused and in control, and Thomas and Dominic were treading effortlessly. Meanwhile, I was trying hard to control my breathing and even harder to motivate my muscles to keep on going.

"Eight minutes!" Pirate Pete called, looking at his stopwatch.

By then I was already counting the seconds, one all the way up to sixty, again and again. I stopped looking at everyone else and kept my eyes on the water in front of me. I ignored the ache of my body and pictured myself diving to Cetus, finding the perfect shell for Raelyn at the bottom of the sea, sleeping in a bunk with a view of the fish and night-time sea creatures. Luciana Vega: Cetus diver. Luciana Vega: first girl to Mars.

I didn't look up until I heard Claire say, "Ella? Are you okay?".

Ella had sunk lower into the water, her ears nearly submerged.

"Ella?" I called breathlessly.

When her ears dipped underwater, I called out her name again, but she still didn't answer. Knowing Ella, she'd rather drown than fail a test. But then Sarah swooped in and helped her to the side of the pool.

Claire looked at me, frowning. "Is she okay?" She wasn't even out of breath.

"I . . . hope . . ." I sputtered, but it was the best I could do with the little air I had left in my lungs. But I was pretty sure Ella was *not* okay. This skills test was probably the first test in her entire life that she didn't pass.

When the stopwatch buzzer went off, we all swam back to the ledge, breathing heavily, our muscles tired, but I was happy and relieved that I passed the first test.

Sarah and Marcus and Pirate Pete gave us high fives. "You passed! Good job!"

I couldn't help noticing Ella sitting red-faced on the bench, wrapped in a towel, her hair dripping on the floor. Her arms were crossed tightly over her chest.

I climbed out of the pool. "Ella? Are you okay? Don't worry you'll—"

"I'm not worried," she said in a yelling kind of voice.

Sensing tension, everyone looked over in our direction as they dried off and collected their things. The boys headed down the ramp without a word.

"I meant—"

"Can we go now?" she snapped, throwing her towel on the ground, and racing down the pool ramp.

Claire tossed her wet towel in the bin and took off after Ella. Picking up Ella's towel, I walked to the bin with mixed emotions. I was two skills tests away from possibly making the dive team.

But what about Ella?

CHAPTER 5

PAIRING UP

On the way back to our cottage, Claire tried to offer Ella lots of tips about treading water. But if I'd learned anything about Ella at Space Camp, it was that offering this kind of advice was not the best idea. Ella was more of the figure-it-out-by-herself kind of girl.

"Were you doing the right type of kick?" Claire continued her prodding.

I couldn't even catch up with Ella, who was power walking through the grassy area, trying to lose Claire.

But Claire only talked louder. "I remember once when my dad was building this rocket that cost him like a trillion dollars," she half shouted to Ella, "and it just wasn't working right. He told me that you have to keep trying. When you really want something, you don't give up on the first try."

If I was being honest, it was pretty good advice.

Except her timing was not the greatest, according to the scowl on Ella's face.

"I'm not giving up if that's what you're saying," Ella said, turning around. And then, to my surprise, she softened a bit, even slowing down for a second. "Sorry. It's just . . . I'm not that kind of person."

But then she raced off to the cottage, closing herself in the bathroom by the time Claire and I got inside. She didn't even come with us to lunch, which was a shame because they had watermelon and I happened to know that was her favorite.

If it was Raelyn, I would have packed up some watermelon for her and we would have eaten it together and talked all about what happened in the pool. With Ella, it was best to just give her some time when she was angry or upset.

And even later that afternoon when we all met back in the hangar for our partner projects, I could tell Ella wasn't feeling much better, sitting rigid and straight-faced in her chair. She didn't even save a seat for me next to her at the big conference table, so I sat across from her.

"Ella," I called to her in a whisper. "Are you okay?"

"I'm fine," she said.

I sat back and left her alone, reminding myself that Ella just needed to come around on her own.

"Welcome back, Cetus Team," Sarah said. "You had a great showing in the pool this morning, and now it's time to start thinking about partner projects. Over the next two weeks you'll work with a partner on a project that will be used on board Cetus during the diving team's mission. You'll each become experts in your area."

"Two of you will build an underwater robot to perform a task on the sea floor," Marcus said. "Another set of partners will use the 3-D printer to create kitchen utensils and an all-purpose tool we can use while on Cetus. And the third group will grow hydroponic plants for food."

Buzz raised his hand, waving it. "Can I make the robot?"

Marcus placed a basket full of little slips of paper on the table. "To be fair to everyone, we're going to randomly assign jobs," Marcus said. He slid the basket over to Buzz. "Here, pick a paper."

Buzz sighed. "If I get boring plants, I'm going to . . ." He read his paper. "3-D printing expert." He shrugged. "Okay."

He passed the basket to Thomas, who selected a slip. "Robotics expert." Thomas grinned. "Cool."

Buzz hit his head against the table. "Come on!"

Dominic picked robotics too, and when it was my turn, I got hydroponics expert, which made me happy. I come from a gardening family. My mom likes to grow fresh herbs and flowers in our backyard, and my abuelita's patio back in Chile is like one big flower garden.

Claire got hydroponics expert too, waving her little slip of paper around, and surprise-attacking me with a hug. "I'm already such an expert on growing stuff hydroponically!"

Okay . . . I thought.

That meant Ella would work with Buzz at the 3-D printer. She slumped from across the table. If it were up to me, I'd take Buzz for a partner over braggy, expert hydroponics-grower Claire any day.

Everyone moved to their stations. Buzz and Ella's 3-D printer stood next to a table where a dozen or so Rocket Science campers were building something big out of soda bottles. Claire and I ducked into the greenhouse, which was basically a large tent made from a semitransparent plastic tarp. The greenhouse shelves were stocked with garden supplies and science equipment. Claire grabbed two official-looking lab coats from a hook and tossed one to me.

I opened a binder on the metal table in front of us that said, "Protocols," and flipped to the "Setting Up" page.

"I'm not used to following protocols," Claire said after she read the book title. "I can usually just figure things out. Same with my dad. It's genetic or something."

I stopped reading for a second. "Are you the kid that skipped to college?" I asked.

"No, I went to the Arctic with my dad." She shook her head, laughing. "I probably *could* have skipped to college, though," she continued, brushing her hair out of her face and putting on a pair of lab goggles, "but I figure, why rush?"

Ignoring her comment, I moved my finger down the list of materials. "Well, when you're doing science stuff, everyone should follow the protocol," I told her. "I mean, if you just skip ahead because you think you know everything, you might miss something important, right?" Immediately, I wished I hadn't said that. "That came out wrong, I meant—"

"It's okay," Claire said with a smile. "I think I know what you mean."

Maybe she did. And maybe I had to give her a chance. After all, Ella seemed to like her. Although, I admit, I couldn't figure out why Ella was so impressed by her. Anyway, we were roommates and teammates and that counted for a lot.

"Okay," I said, returning to the list. "We need the plant pillows, seeds, and a beaker filled with water."

"Have you ever used one of these turkey basters before?" Claire asked me, inspecting a small glass tube with a rubber bulb stuck to the top.

"You mean a 'pipette'?" I asked. "Yeah, I saw these in the plant lab at Space Camp." Shouldn't Claire-the-hydroponics-expert already know what the tools are called?

Claire squared her shoulders. "Of course I know it's a pipette," she said. "I just didn't think you'd have any idea what I was talking about."

I bristled, but decided it wasn't worth making a big deal out of it. We searched for our supplies in the cabinets and glass cooler in the corner of the greenhouse. I found a bunch of butter lettuce seeds and Claire found the plant pillows, which looked a lot like the travel pack of wipes Mom kept in her purse for Isadora.

"What's in these anyway?" Claire asked, squishing one of the pillows.

I snapped on a pair of latex gloves. "Stuff to make the plants grow, I guess."

I picked up a pillow and peeked through the tiny hole in the top where we'd insert the lettuce seed. All I saw inside was darkness, but I could smell something earthy, like soil or sand.

"It says 'growth media made out of fertilizer and clay,'" she said, reading from the binder. She wrinkled her nose and tossed the pillow onto the table. "Gross."

What kind of hydroponics expert is grossed out by fertilizer? I wondered. I filled the beaker with water from the jug on the table. "So, you said you've done this before?" I asked. "Like with your dad or something?"

"Probably," she said, tearing open a seed packet. "Or maybe not. I can't remember."

I eyed her. So, maybe she wasn't an expert on hydroponics after all.

"Sometimes I garden with my mom," I said. "But

we do regular gardening in our backyard, so I'm new to hydroponics."

Claire didn't say anything, looking at our next step in the protocol. "Hand me that?" she said, pointing to a Styrofoam tray. I slid it over to her and she dumped the seeds into it. "We need to put three into each plant pillow."

She put on some latex gloves and we got to work, dropping three tiny seeds into each pillow. Through the foggy plastic tarp we could see and hear the other teams working outside the greenhouse. The Rocket Science kids were the loudest as they put together their giant rocket and when they finally went outside, the hangar seemed to echo with quietness.

Sarah poked her head in. "You two doing okay?"

Claire held up a seed with her gloved hand. "Planting."

Sarah inspected our setup. "Good job, guys. Keep it up and we'll be eating fresh butter lettuce salad for dinner on Cetus."

"Really?" I said. "So fast?"

"Yep." Sarah nodded. "Hydroponic plants grow faster because instead of growing in regular soil, they get a mixture of nutrients just perfect for the plant. They don't have to spend time growing a big root system because everything they need is right there in the growth media."

"That makes sense," Claire said.

"There's no soil on Mars or on the ISS, so astronauts have turned to hydroponics. You could grow a plant anywhere if you don't have to rely on soil," Sarah said.

She watched us plant a few more seeds and then disappeared back out the flap door.

Claire and I continued working silently. I wanted to ask her a thousand questions about what it was like to be Lance Jacobs's daughter. Did they live in a huge mansion? Was she going to be the first girl to Mars? Did they eat space food for dinner and fly famous astronauts around in their helicopter all the time? Because, that's probably what I would do if I were her.

"If I had a helicopter, I'd fly it right to Chile," I accidentally said out loud.

She looked up from her plant pillow. "We did that once. We took our jet, though. My dad had something to do in the Atacama Desert."

I dropped a seed, thinking about my family, and it skittered across the table. "My abuelita lives there and also some cousins. I never get to see them."

"Actually, maybe I didn't go to Chile that time. I probably had homework or something." She finished her planting and pushed the Styrofoam tray away.

So, she *hadn't* been to Chile? Or had she?

I shook my head, reading the next step. "Add 100 mL of water to each plant pillow."

Claire raised up the pipette. "Turkey baster thingy." She submerged the glass tube into the beaker, squeezing the bulb and drawing in water until it reached the little line on the tube that read "100 mL." And then she squeezed the bulb hard, squirting the water into one of the pillows. She handed it to me. "Your turn."

I moved the plant pillow closer to me and sat down on a stool so I could really concentrate. If we were on the real space station, where water and supplies were limited, one mistake and an entire experiment could be ruined. At first I squeezed the bulb too hard and sucked up too much water. Claire laughed, but in a nice kind of way, not the making-fun-of-me kind of way.

I tried again, this time going slower, and managed to get it right. Claire and I took turns adding water to the rest of the plant pillows.

"Do you get to go places with your dad a lot?" I asked, wondering if that's what life would be like if my mom or dad had decided to be a space entrepreneur like Lance Jacobs instead of a nurse and math teacher.

"Well, he usually travels without me," Claire said, pulling up some water with the pipette. She looked up suddenly, her cheeks turning a little pink. "I mean, not like he doesn't want me there. But if it's a place too dangerous for a twelve-year-old or something then I probably wouldn't go." She passed me the pipette. "He's always home for Halloween, though. That's his favorite holiday."

"That's cool, I guess," I said, adding water to the last pillow.

"Anyway, inventors and company presidents have to travel a lot and my dad is both of those things." She peeled her gloves off and tossed them in the trash. "It's the reality of the situation, you know?"

I nodded, trying to read Claire's face, but I couldn't figure out what she was thinking.

Following the last steps of the protocol, we carefully loaded our plant pillows into the growing tray in the corner of the greenhouse. Then we put on protective sunglasses and flipped on the panel of lights, bathing ourselves in the glow of the red, blue, and green LEDs.

"Awesome," Claire said, and it was.

We started cleaning up, and I peered at Claire as she dumped the water out of the beaker and placed the glass tube from the pipette in the biohazard bin.

I was having a hard time figuring out exactly what was real and was not real with Claire. It seemed as though when Claire wasn't bragging, she was making up stories.

I took a breath. *We are on the same team. We are roommates,* I reminded myself. Sarah said we'd be family by the end of the week.

So, I let my bad feelings go. This time.

CHAPTER 6

LEFT OUT

The next morning, I awoke to Sarah tapping on the cabin window, letting us know it was time to get up for breakfast. Groggily, I wiped my hair out of my face and hung over the side of my bed. "Good mor—"

But Claire's and Ella's bunks were empty and their beds were even made as if they'd been up for hours.

"Ella? Claire?" I jumped down and quickly got dressed before stumbling outside. Thomas and Dominic were sitting with Sarah in the grassy area by the beach, watching the water. Buzz was just leaving his own cabin, blinking in the bright sun.

"Has anyone seen my roommates?" I asked, sitting next to Thomas.

"They're working in the pool with one of the lifeguards," Sarah said, stretching her legs. "Claire was kind enough to offer to train Ella in the pool each morning to help her catch up to the rest of the group."

Buzz collapsed into the spot on the grass next to me, flopping over and closing his eyes.

"Teamwork," Sarah said. "Sacrificing for the greater good of the mission, you know?" She nudged Buzz with her shoe.

But it didn't feel like teamwork if not everyone was included. And sneaking out of the cottage before all the teammates were up? That didn't feel like teamwork either. Claire and Ella left me out. I ran my fingers through my hair, spotting my purple stripe, and thought of Raelyn. We always included everyone. It was basically one of our rules.

I felt a streak of loneliness and wished I could call Raelyn, but I knew she was at art camp already. My heart was suddenly heavy with homesickness.

"Are we allowed to call home today?" I asked, knowing my parents were probably up with Isadora already.

"Of course," Sarah said. "We've set up the video-chat app on the laptop by the 3-D printer." She stood up. "Come find me after breakfast and I'll get you started."

After Sarah walked away, Buzz popped up. "I'm getting in line for bacon." He ran toward the dining hall.

Dominic pulled out a pair of binoculars, scanning

the beach. Across the calm water of the Chesapeake Bay was Assateague Island. If I squinted, I could make out a few wild horses eating their breakfast of marshy grasses on the shore.

"I was going to ask Sarah the same question about calling home," Thomas said. "I miss my family too."

I perked up. "You do?" I asked, surprised, because I thought I was the only kid here who felt homesick.

"A ton," he said with a sad smile.

And for some reason just knowing he felt the same way made me feel less alone.

"I have a baby sister," I told him. "She needs surgery on her heart."

Thomas sat up straighter. "Oh. Wow. That's . . . but she's okay?"

Dominic put his binoculars down. "My uncle had surgery on his heart and we bought him a balloon and his favorite cookies at the hospital. But the doctor said he couldn't eat the cookies because they aren't good for people who have heart surgery, I guess."

I sighed. Isadora loved cookies. But maybe a balloon would make her just as happy after her surgery.

Thomas was looking at me, still waiting for me to

answer his question. "My parents said she'll be okay," I said, shrugging because how could they even know if that was true?

"Hey, guys." Claire and Ella walked up to us, their hair still dripping wet from the pool. "Did you see we have our first scuba lesson this morning?" Claire asked.

Ella waved to me, looking more cheerful today. "Claire's helping me train to pass my next treading water test. I got up to nine minutes!"

"Oh, and good news," Claire said. "Even though Ella failed the treading test, Sarah said she can do the scuba lesson today."

I saw Ella's ears turn a little red.

"Well, I can help in the pool tomorrow if you want," I offered.

"That's okay," Claire said. "We got special permission, and I've been doing this kind of thing for my whole life, almost. I've trained a ton of people."

"She's a really good teacher," Ella said, nodding.

I pushed away my left-out feelings and all the other mixed-up feelings I had about Claire, and managed a smile. "That sounds great," I said.

Thomas had taken a turn looking at the ponies with Dominic's binoculars, and now he handed them to me.

To my disappointment, the ponies had left the shore, so instead I focused on the beach by our yellow cottage where tiny snails and hermit crabs scooched around on the wet sand. They made me think of Raelyn and how when we were little we spent hours scooping them into our pails to keep them as pets until our parents made us put them back.

"Thanks," I said, handing the binoculars back to Dominic, my homesickness welling up again. "I'm going to call my family. I'll see you guys at the pool, okay?" I said to Ella and Claire.

"Say hi to Izzy for me," Ella said as Claire hooked her elbow and dragged her back to the cottage.

I grabbed a bagel in the cafeteria and then went to find Sarah. I found her at a table finishing up her breakfast, and together we walked to the hangar, stepping around the Aviation kids lined up on the lawn for calisthenics.

Sarah opened up the video-chat application on the laptop and entered my dad's cell phone number. "This is how the astronauts on the International Space Station talk to their family members while they're gone. So, that's how we do it here too," Sarah said as I scarfed down the second half of my bagel. I was excited to see

Isadora, even if it was on a computer screen. Anything was better than nothing.

"We have scuba skills in a few minutes," Sarah reminded me, "so don't stay on too long. You can meet us at the pool when you're done."

"Okay," I said. A few minutes was all I needed. Anyway, I already had my bathing suit under my clothes.

When the chat first connected, all I saw was Dad's hand in the webcam, but then came Isadora's little face. "Lulululululuuuuu!" she squealed when she saw me. "Lululu!"

I waved and waved. But I wanted to hug her and kiss her sweet face, and I wasn't sure if calling home was making anything better, feeling my heart pang even harder. "Where's your penguin?"

Isadora pushed away from Dad and toddled out of the picture.

"How are you doing at camp, Luci?" Dad asked, turning to me. "Are you having a great time? How is Ella?"

"Ella is doing great," I said, leaving out the part about her failing the treading test. Although she seemed to be doing great with her new friend. "How is Izzy?"

"Hi, honey! We had an appointment with the surgeon this morning," Mom said, popping into the picture, "and she said Izzy's doing okay but if a spot opens up before our scheduled surgery, she'd like us to take it."

"What?" I twirled my hair, sitting up straighter. "She wants Izzy to have her surgery early? Like, before I even get home from camp?"

"It's nothing to worry about, sweetheart," Dad said. "If they can get her in earlier, it would be better. If anything changes, we'll call you right away, okay?"

"Wait," I said. "So, if there's an opening tomorrow, Izzy will take it?"

"Yes," Dad said. "But for now we want you to focus on having fun at camp."

"I'll try," I said, not liking this new plan. Because now it felt like an emergency type of surgery. "But will you promise to call me the minute you get the new date?"

"As soon as we find out," Mom said.

Before I knew it, the bell to start camp sessions chimed. I had to go. We said our good-byes, and I waved and clapped for Isadora who brought me her penguin, and then when no one was looking, I kissed the screen. And so did Isadora. And so did her penguin.

CHAPTER 7

THUMBS-UP,
THUMBS-DOWN

When I got to the pool, I tried to put all of my Isadora worries and bad feelings from the morning behind me. I had to get serious if I wanted to make the dive team. I focused my attention on Pirate Pete, who was showing us the hand signals that we should use to communicate while diving, like the A-OK sign, and the watch-out-there's-a-boat sign, and the out-of-air sign.

"It's not like you're cutting your own neck off," Pete said to the boys doing their own violent version of the out-of-air sign. "Like this." He moved his hand from one shoulder to the other.

"So, I can't do a thumbs-up to say, like, 'good-job' anymore?" Dominic said.

"When you're scuba diving, a thumbs-up means you need to surface. Thumbs-down means you're ready to go under," Pirate Pete said, grabbing a wire basket off the shelf. "Come pick a scuba mask and let's get in the water."

"Do we need flippers?" Buzz said, standing next to a container full of them.

Pirate Pete chuckled, and so did I. "Those are called fins, and no, not today."

Buzz sighed and lowered himself into the pool. Ella tapped me on the shoulder, her green scuba mask pulled up onto her head. "Hey, want to practice in the pool tomorrow with us? It's super fun and Claire will tell you all about the time she scuba dived in the Bahamas with a ton of sharks."

I took a pink scuba mask from Pirate Pete. Hearing Claire's diving stories that may or may not have been totally true did not sound like my idea of a great way to start the day. "Maybe." But when I thought about it more, I figured it would be better than hanging out by myself. "Okay, probably."

"Great!" she said. "Sorry I didn't wake you up this morning. I should have asked if you wanted to come too."

My heart swelled because just hearing her say that made me feel not so left out anymore. "Thanks, Ella."

Once our crew was in the water, Pirate Pete, now fully decked out in scuba diving gear, showed us how to adjust our masks. Claire swam over to Ella and me and we all dunked ourselves and waved and gave our A-OK signs to one another.

Ella and I popped out of the water at the same time.

"I can see all the way to the bottom. It's so clear!" I said.

Ella nodded, a big smile on her face.

Once we were all set with our masks, Marcus and Sarah came over to the side of the pool holding scuba vests with air tanks strapped to the back. Buzz got his first, lines and gauges and tubes floating out from behind him like an octopus.

"Regulator." Pirate Pete held up a long tube with a round piece of equipment and a mouthpiece attached to the end. "This is what you breathe through. Try it." He placed it in his mouth and so did Buzz, who was looking more serious than I'd ever seen.

Marcus put an air tank on Dominic and then Thomas and Sarah brought over three sets of scuba tanks to Claire, Ella, and me.

Sarah held up a vest for me, and I put it on, zipping into it and tightening all the straps. But when she let go of the air tanks on my back, I was so surprised by how heavy they were that I tripped backward in the water. Ella grabbed me before I fell into the deep part of the pool.

"Should kids even be doing this?" Buzz yelled from across the platform, holding his regulator up.

"Scuba diving?" Pirate Pete said. "Yes, kids are fine to be scuba diving."

"That's what I thought," Buzz said. "Just checking in case anyone wasn't sure." He peeled off his air tanks and pulled himself onto the pool deck. "Bathroom break. Don't wait for me!"

We practiced breathing through our mouthpieces above and under the water, all of us standing in a line in front of Pirate Pete. At first it felt uncomfortable, as if I wasn't getting enough oxygen. But then I got used to it and soon we were all kneeling on the underwater platform, breathing through our regulators like professional scuba divers. All except for Buzz who was still taking his bathroom break.

Still underwater, Pirate Pete signaled to us to watch him. Then he grabbed his scuba mask with both hands and tipped it forward, filling it with water. Then he showed us how to clear all the water from the mask by blowing bubbles through his nose, forcing the water out of the bottom of his mask. He pointed to us, telling us to try it. I looked at Claire, who filled up her mask and expelled the water in one try.

Pirate Pete pointed to me next. I took a deep breath through my regulator and tilted my mask forward. The water rushed into my mask so cold and fast, I felt stunned for a second. And even though I'd had water in my goggles at the pool before, it felt more dangerous and serious when you were all dressed up in scuba gear. I got some water in my nose and I came up fast, coughing and sputtering and choking.

Ella came up too. "Are you okay?"

I yanked off my scuba mask and took deep breaths, my nose still stinging from the water.

"Want me to show you how—" Claire started, but I shook my head. I could do this. If I wanted to go to Cetus, I wasn't going to let a little water in my mask get in my way.

I went under again and filled up my mask, taking careful breaths only through my regulator. I pressed my hand to the top of my mask and blew bubbles hard through my nose. There was a little bit of water still left at the bottom of my mask so I blew again, concentrating on breathing through my regulator at the same time. Ella and Claire clapped for me underwater. I did it!

Ella had no trouble blowing the water out of her mask. In fact, she got it right the first time. Pirate Pete gave us all A-OK signs and then a thumbs-up. We surfaced, the boys still practicing their skill.

"Great job. That was part one of the scuba skills," he said.

"That's it?" I said, grinning at Ella and Claire. "We passed?"

Marcus and Sarah clapped from where they sat on the side of the pool, their legs dangling in the water.

"Yes, you passed the first part. That's a hard technique for many people," Marcus said. "You really have to talk your body into feeling calm, even though your face is covered with water. Okay, you three are ready to learn the second part. If you get this right, then you pass your scuba skills and you'll be ready to do the pool dive on Sunday."

Claire raised her hand. "But not if you haven't passed the treading water test, right? I mean, I have but . . ."

Ella's cheeks went bright red.

"We'll give everyone the chance to make up any tests before the dive," Pirate Pete said.

"Good," Claire said, looking at Ella. "It's such an easy test; there's no way you won't pass."

"It's not that easy," I said. "Treading water is hard work." And then I stopped talking because from the look on Ella's face, I probably wasn't helping the situation.

"We'd make great candidates for the dive team, huh?" I said, trying to change the subject.

Marcus and Sarah laughed. "Let's see how you do on this next part, Miss Confidence."

Ella grabbed my hand and squeezed it, smiling, and then to my surprise, Claire took my other hand and it felt nice, the three of us standing there swinging our arms back and forth together while we waited for instructions from Pete.

"It's a little bit weird that you, me, and Ella are all on the same crew," Claire said to me, "but at the same time also competing against one another."

I squinted at her. "What?" I asked, because that was the opposite of what I was thinking. "I'm hoping we all get picked for the team. Together."

Ella looked from Claire to me. "I think what Claire meant is that it's kind of unfair how the whole crew can't go to Cetus, right?"

"Yeah, sure." Claire nodded her head. "That's totally what I meant." And then she whipped her wet ponytail over her shoulder, spraying me.

Pirate Pete clapped his hands together. "Okay, next up: What is a pirate's favorite class?"

Sarah groaned. "Feel free not to answer that."

Ella shot her hand into the air. "Arrrrrrrt class!"

Pete slapped the water with his hand, chuckling and we couldn't help cracking up a little too.

"But seriously," he said, getting back to business. "In the event of an emergency, like you're out of air or your regulator has malfunctioned, you'll need to share air with your dive buddy." He reached for the hose on his back. It held a second regulator.

"Oh, this is easy. I've done this a ton of times," Claire said.

Another story. I wanted to roll my eyes, but Claire had proven herself with the first scuba skills tests, so I decided to give her the benefit of the doubt.

"When you take your own regulator out of your mouth, do not hold your breath. Instead blow a small, steady stream of bubbles through your lips." He turned to Claire. "Let's demonstrate." And then he flashed a thumbs-down sign and we went underwater, kneeling on the platform.

Pete gave Claire an A-OK sign. She took out her regulator, swam over to Pete while blowing bubbles, and took his emergency regulator. She put it in her mouth, pressed the button to expel the water in the lines, and started breathing like no big deal. *Okay, so maybe Claire wasn't lying about diving with the sharks in the Bahamas,* I said to myself.

Pete pointed to Ella. She spit out her mouthpiece and easily took my extra air hose. Dominic and Thomas were still taking the first part of the scuba skills, so Pirate Pete moved closer to them so he could better see us all. Once Ella was breathing off of my emergency regulator, he gave her the A-OK sign and then pointed to me and Claire.

I pulled out my regulator, and moved over to Claire, and when I realized her emergency hose was on the other side of her air tanks, I tried swimming around her but got out of breath too fast and had to surface.

"You all right?" Marcus said from the side of the pool.

I nodded, putting my own regulator back in and trying again. This time I lined up on the right side of Claire before removing my air. But still, before I could snag Claire's emergency regulator, I ran out of breath from blowing bubbles out of my mouth, and came sputtering out of the water again.

Claire came up this time. "Do you need a break?"

It was almost as if she was moving away from me underwater. I'd never had trouble losing my breath underwater before. In fact, Raelyn and I always played how-long-can-you-stay-underwater games at the pool and I won every time.

"Nope, I can do this," I told Claire.

"I need to take a bathroom break," Ella said. "Are you sure you can do this test now, Luci? Maybe you need a break too."

I shook my head. "No, thanks. I can do this." Then I turned to Claire. "Ready?" The two of us went underwater again. This time I swam a bit closer to Claire before taking out my regulator. But, again, I ran out of air before I could reach her emergency mouthpiece. What was even happening? I swam up to surface, gasping.

When Claire came up she said, "Maybe you do need that break."

"No," I said, "I'm doing this today."

I looked at the pool's edge and I could have sworn we had just been standing in front of the filter, which was now at least two feet away. I was right. Claire *had* moved away from me. Just enough so I couldn't quite reach her regulator.

Hadn't she?

"Maybe you're not ready for this skills test," Claire suggested.

Was she serious? "I'm definitely ready for this test, Claire," I said.

Ella came back from the bathroom, her goggles pushed up on her head.

"Did you figure it out?" she asked, pointing to Claire's emergency regulator.

I shook my head.

"Just because we made it look so simple, doesn't mean it is, right, Ella?" Claire said.

I was practically vibrating with anger.

"You moved away from me," I snapped. "We started all the way down there." I waved to the pool filter. "And now we're over here. How did that happen if you weren't moving away from me?"

"What?" Claire said. "That's ridiculous. Ella, you were right with us the first time, did I move away from her?"

"Oh, um . . ." Ella glanced at me. "Sorry, I got distracted watching the boys do their mask skill, and then I was just in the bathroom, and . . ."

"Time's up," Pirate Pete interrupted, glancing at his

waterproof watch. "Don't forget that if you didn't pass a skill today, you have until Friday to make it up. You'll have lots of time over the next few days to practice and catch up."

"Can I have another minute, Pirate Pete?" I asked. "I want to try one more time." I glared at Claire.

"Okay," Pete said. "But let's make it quick. There's another group scheduled to use the pool in a few minutes."

This time Pirate Pete came under with us and miraculously, I was able to reach Claire's emergency regulator right away, barely getting out of breath.

When we reached the surface, Claire and Ella bounced up and down for me, making little waves in the pool.

"It doesn't matter how many times it takes," Claire said to me. "You did a great job."

And I tried to smile. I really did. But I couldn't get out of my head what Claire had said earlier. About how we all wanted a spot on the dive team and that made us competitors instead of teammates. Was she competing against me instead of treating me like a teammate? Is that why she moved away?

Or was it all in my head?

CHAPTER 8

SEEDLING

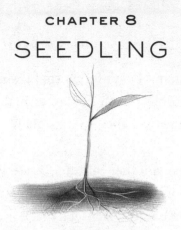

The next morning, Ella woke me up early, the sky still pink with sunrise. "We're going to the pool. Want to come?" But they were already dressed and Claire was halfway out the door, the humid bay air floating into our cottage.

I sat up in bed. "Pete said we'll have time to practice in the pool later today. Why are you up so early?"

"I have to pass this, Luci."

"Yeah, I know," I said. This treading test was why Ella was so good at not failing at things. She practiced until she got it right.

Claire was getting impatient, shifting her weight from one leg to the other at the door. "I can train you with some scuba stuff too, Luci."

I pasted on a smile, but I really didn't feel like spending any more time in the pool with Claire after what happened yesterday. "Thanks, but I think I'm doing okay," I said.

As soon as Claire closed the door to wait outside, I leaned over the bed. "I don't trust her," I whispered to Ella as she tied her shoes. I couldn't hold it in any longer.

"Who? Claire?" Ella said like it was the most ridiculous thing she had ever heard.

"Yes," I said firmly.

"Because she offered to help train you?" Ella said, standing up. "She's just trying to help. Because honestly it took you a long time to pass the second part of the skills test yesterday."

Anger flared in my belly, and I pushed all my covers off. "Because she kept moving away from me!"

Ella shook her head. "Why would she do that? And anyway, she already said she didn't."

"And we should just believe her?"

Ella sighed. It was obvious we did not have the same kind of feelings about Claire.

"It doesn't matter. I've already passed all my skills tests, no thanks to her," I said more softly.

Ella crossed her arms over her chest. "In case you forgot, not all of us have passed our skills tests."

"I didn't mean it like that, Ella."

She turned to the door.

"I'm sorry," I said. "Look, I just don't think she's a good friend."

She looked back at me. "Maybe *you're* the one not being a good friend."

I sat up, shocked by her sharp words.

She dropped her shoulders. "Wait, no. Luci, I'm sorry. I didn't mean that. It's just, Claire's not so bad, you know?" Ella said. "You should give her a chance so we can all be friends."

I felt a knot in my belly. Giving people a chance was practically my specialty, but there was something about Claire. Taking my bed that first night, and the left-out feeling I had when I was around her and Ella. Plus, I really did think she moved away from me in the pool. But instead of saying something and making Ella upset again, I said, "All right." And I gave her an A-OK sign and watched her head out of the cabin.

I ate breakfast with Thomas, Dominic, and Buzz under a tree by the beach.

"Where were you during the scuba lesson yester-day?" I asked Buzz, whose mouth was full of biscuits dipped in honey. "You missed the skills tests."

"Nurse," Buzz said, wiping his face with a napkin. "Too much bacon I think."

Buzz took another bite of biscuit and didn't say anything else. I got the sense that he wasn't telling the whole truth, but I let it go.

Once we finished breakfast, we headed back to the hangar to work on our projects. I was relieved when Ella smiled and waved at me from her spot in front of the 3-D printer as she sorted through a bunch of colored plastic filament with Buzz. I really didn't want to fight with her and decided then and there that I would try my hardest to give Claire another chance—for Ella's sake.

When I headed over to the greenhouse, Claire was already there in her lab coat and goggles.

"No sprouts yet," she said, inspecting one of the plant pillows.

"We should probably add another 100 milliliters of water," I suggested.

She flipped the UV light off and started lining up the plant pillows on a tray to move them over to the metal worktable. I filled a beaker with water from the jug and pulled out a pipette, pushing the rubber bulb onto the end of the glass tube.

"What was it like to dive in the Bahamas?" I asked, trying to make friendly conversation.

Her face lit up. "It was the best. It was so clear. I saw so many fish. There was even a nurse shark that liked swimming around the boat, but the captain told me not to worry because they aren't mean. When my dad came back to the surface, he brought me a giant conch shell." She handed me the pipette to take my turn. "It was this huge." She held her hands out wide.

"You didn't go to the bottom with him?"

She shook her head. "I was only eight. They don't let eight-year-olds scuba dive." She laughed, like this was everyday common knowledge.

"But I thought you said—"

"I was with my dad for all the training, though," she continued, "and they let me watch and try some stuff out in the pool. So, technically, I haven't been diving yet, but it was pretty much the same thing."

No, I thought, it was not the same thing. But I took a breath, remembering what Ella said about wanting us all to be friends. I wanted that too. I just needed to try a little harder. *I suppose watching her dad dive gives her more experience than I have,* I told myself.

"When I go to Cetus, my dad said he'll fly in to dive down to the habitat with me," Claire said, taking her turn with the pipette.

"You mean *if* you make the dive team?" I corrected her.

Claire smiled. "Right. Of course. But don't you think the team is going to be you, me, and Dominic?"

I stood up, bringing the watered plants back to the growing area. "But what about Ella? She's been practicing so much."

"I know," Claire said, putting her sunglasses on and turning on the UV light bank. "I told her she's doing great and all, but the honest truth is that I worry she's just not good enough yet."

"She'll be ready," I said, because clearly Claire didn't know the real Ella. The not-giving-up kind of Ella. "Who knows? Maybe it will be you, me, and Ella on the dive team."

Claire clapped. "That would be perfect."

I hoped she meant it.

It seemed like watering the plants really helped because the next day a little shoot of green peeked up through one of the plant pillows. Our first sprout.

"It's so cute," Claire said, both of us leaning over the growing area. "So delicate."

We brought it to our greenhouse table, and I measured it with a ruler. Our tiny bit of butter lettuce was one centimeter tall. Claire pulled out the protocol binder and tore out an observation sheet, giving me the honor of making our first entry. I recorded the size and shape of our sprout and the bright green color.

"Want to take the picture?" I asked, handing Claire the lab camera. It looked like an ordinary camera except when Claire pressed the button, an instant photo of our little seedling popped out.

"Cool," I said, taping it onto our observation sheet. "Perfect."

"One more," Claire said. She held the camera out, and took one of us, smiling with our baby sprout, and when we got back to our cottage that night, we hung it up on the wall.

And even though I still had some doubts about Claire, I had to admit that we looked like real friends.

CHAPTER 9

MAKING WAVES

On Friday, Claire, Dominic, and I sat on the side of the pool with our feet dangling in the water. The three of us had passed all of our skills tests and were ready for the big dive to the bottom of the pool on Sunday. We were there to cheer on Ella, Thomas, and Buzz as they tried to pass their tests.

While Ella was in the changing room, Thomas was on the platform, ready to retake the scuba mask skills test.

"You've got this, Thomas!" Dominic called, and Thomas gave him an A-OK sign.

Buzz was lingering by the racks of gear, clutching his stomach.

Thomas dipped under the water. Moments later, he sprang up, coughing and sputtering, his mask still full of water. He tore it off.

"You can do it!" shouted Dominic.

Thomas tried again, and when he came back up, he spit out his regulator, grinning.

Pirate Pete held up one of Thomas's arms like he had just won a boxing match. "Winner!"

Sarah helped a dripping and shivering Thomas out of his scuba gear.

"Who's next?" Pete asked.

"Me!" Ella said, coming out of the dressing room.

She was ready to do this skills test. I could see it in the way she walked across the pool platform. She knew she had it this time. As Ella waded into the pool with Pirate Pete, Marcus escorted a very pale-looking Buzz to the ramp.

"Where are you going?" Dominic asked as Buzz and Marcus walked past us. "You have like a thousand skills tests to make up."

"Nurse," he groaned. "Bacon."

"Really?" Dominic said. "Again?"

"I just can't resist the stuff."

Marcus led him to the ramp back down to the floor of the hangar.

"Since Marcus is helping Buzz, can someone else be in charge of timing for me so I can get this stuff put away?" Sarah asked, lining up Thomas's gear and getting ready to sanitize everything and store it in the racks.

Claire hopped up. "I'll do it!"

Sarah reached into a bin, pulled out a stopwatch, and handed it to Claire.

"Set it to countdown from fifteen," Sarah instructed, watching Claire get it all set up. "There. Good. Hang it from your neck so you don't drop it."

But Claire was barely listening, skipping back to the rest of us at the side of the pool with the stopwatch in her hand. "You ready, Ella?"

Ella nodded and Pete held up three fingers and we counted down together. "Three . . . two . . . one . . . go!"

Claire started the stopwatch, and Ella pushed off the platform, floating into the deep end. I pretty much started holding my breath, worried. Because what if Claire was right? What if Ella wasn't ready? Thomas sat with us, wrapped in a towel, the four of us swirling our legs through the water. Every few seconds, I peered over Claire's shoulder and watched the countdown on the stopwatch. 14 minutes 34 seconds, 13 minutes 48 seconds . . . until my neck started hurting from the strain of it.

I kept trying to get Ella's attention so I could give

her an A-OK sign. I waved, made funny faces, and even splashed her a bit, but she was too focused.

"How's the robot build going?" I finally asked Thomas after it was quiet for a minute or two, Ella still looking strong in the water.

"We just have a few more tweaks to make but we'll be ready to test him in the pool on Sunday," he said.

The big dive to the bottom of the pool on Sunday was our first chance to practice the tasks we would perform on Cetus, which meant I'd be doing an EVA to take samples from the bottom of the pool, pretending they were samples of sand, and Dominic and Thomas would practice a set of robotic operations and run their robot underwater for the first time.

I looked at the stopwatch again. Only six minutes and four seconds left and Ella was still smiling.

"Good job, Ella!" I cheered.

We stood up to root Ella on together, chanting, "Go, Ella! You can do it!"

As the time passed, I was feeling less and less worried about Ella not making it this time.

Soon Marcus came back with Buzz, who wasn't holding his stomach anymore.

"Feeling better?" Thomas asked him.

Buzz patted his stomach. "I think I'm allergic to bacon. That's what the nurse said, at least. It's not good for the system."

"Or maybe you're allergic to scuba diving?" Dominic said, but Thomas shushed him.

Soon, we noticed Ella start to fade, her head not so high above the water anymore, with still a few more minutes to go.

"Let's do a wave," I suggested to the rest of the crew, hoping to make Ella laugh. "Like at a baseball game. Buzz, you start."

Buzz bowed his head and came up fanning his arms to the ceiling, Dominic following a second later, and then Thomas and me, and finally Claire. But when Claire raised her arms . . . she lost her grip on the stopwatch and it dropped into the pool.

"The timer!" I yelled. Ella looked really tired at this point. Like, sinking below the surface tired.

Sarah looked at the pool and at Claire. "What? How did—you didn't secure it around your neck? That's why there's a cord!"

And then Marcus was leaning over the side of the pool, trying to help Pirate Pete get Ella to the platform, where she stood, breathing hard.

Sarah ran over and fished the timer out of the pool, where thankfully it had landed on the shallow ledge. But I could tell from the look on Sarah's face that it didn't matter anyway. When she held it up, we could all see that the screen was dark.

"Stopwatches and water don't mix," Sarah said, speaking pointedly at Claire. "I told you to wear it around your neck."

"I didn't hear you," Claire said. "It was an accident."

Sarah put her hand on her hip. "Well do you know how many minutes are left on the timer?"

Claire shook her head. "I—I don't know," she stammered. "I wasn't keeping track."

The rest of us stood up, the entire pool area silent, and for a second I thought Ella was going to cry. "Does that mean I didn't pass?"

All of us just stood there looking at one another. How could Claire have let this happen?

"Let me try it again right now," Ella said, but we all knew her muscles were too tired. She'd never make it another fifteen minutes.

"Can't we just assume she passed?" I blurted out. "The last I checked the time, it was so close to zero. She definitely made it."

"But you can't be sure," Claire said. "I mean, what if there was more time left than you thought?"

I turned to her. "But there wasn't, Claire."

She made a sad shrug.

"Unfortunately, Ella," Sarah said, coming to the side of the pool and kneeling down to talk to her, "if we can't be sure of the time, we can't pass you. It's just the rule. For safety."

Ella exhaled. "Does that mean I can't do the dive on Sunday?"

"I'm sorry, Ella," Sarah said. "The Aviation kids have the pool all day tomorrow for an activity, so there's no time for makeups before the pool dive."

My throat felt tight. Ella wasn't going to dive with us.

"Does that mean she has no chance at making the dive team to Cetus?" This was so unfair.

Sarah and Marcus looked at each other. "Normally, yes that would be the case."

"But we'll take a look at the pool schedule," Marcus said. "Maybe there's a window for one more chance at makeups. Buzz needs to pass his skills tests too."

Claire squatted down next to Sarah. "Ella, I am so sorry. You probably made it."

And maybe it was the way she said "I'm sorry" that

didn't really sound sorry at all or how she told me Ella wasn't going to pass her test when it was clear she would have, but like a jolt, I knew Claire dropped the stopwatch on purpose. My heart thumped in my chest. Was she so worried about Ella taking her spot on Cetus that she'd sabotage her friend like that?

I thought about what happened a few days ago and how I could have sworn Claire was moving away from me underwater. On purpose. Trying to make it so I didn't pass *my* skills test. Could she have done the same thing to Ella?

Claire was telling Ella over and over how bad she felt for her, and all of a sudden I couldn't take it.

"Did you do this on purpose?" I asked, so loud I even shocked myself. "So that Ella wouldn't pass?"

Claire dropped Ella's hand. "What? Of course not."

Sarah looked at me. "Luci, it was an honest mistake."

"What if it wasn't?" But there was no way to prove it. Just my gut feeling. A really strong one.

"Luci . . ." Ella said.

"What? She told me the other day how we were all competing against one another and we know how much she wants to go to Cetus and—"

Claire glared at me, burst into tears, and ran out of the pool area.

"Luci," Sarah said. "I know you're upset for Ella, but if you have a problem with another camper, you should come to Marcus or me or Pete next time, okay?"

When I looked at Ella again, she looked mad. "Way to go Luci," she said. "Way to make Claire feel completely awful when none of this was her fault. She's been helping me for three days! Why would she purposely drop the stopwatch in the water?"

I knew why. Because she wanted to go to Cetus.

"It's like you're jealous or something," Ella said, fuming.

"Jealous?" I repeated, so shocked I could barely form my thoughts. "I'm trying to help you."

"I don't need your help, Luci."

"But that's what friends do!" I said. "Why don't you trust me when I tell you she's not a good friend?"

"I guess I . . ." Ella paused. ". . . I just don't. I mean would you after what happened at Space Camp?"

It was like a punch to the gut.

She was talking about how I almost got us sent home from Space Camp when I thought one of the other robotics teams was cheating. We took matters into our own hands and nearly ruined the entire robotics competition for another team. It had been all my idea—and in the end, it turned out I was wrong.

"It's not like that, Ella," I said. "Not this time."

"That's what you always say, Luci." And then she stomped away, everyone else following her, leaving me alone on the pool deck.

CHAPTER 10

CLOUDED OVER

That night our crew took a buggy ride over the dunes to get a glimpse of the International Space Station through a telescope. It would be in view for only four minutes or so.

When we got to the beach, I trailed behind the rest of the group. It was clear that I was the only one who didn't think Claire was amazing and awesome and the best kid who ever lived. Nobody invited me to share a seat on their driftwood, and when Sarah and Marcus told everyone to quickly line up to see the space station, I kept getting bumped from the line until I was the very last person.

Sarah and Marcus were talking about something up at the front of the line, but with the wind and the waves, it was hard to hear.

I tapped Thomas on the shoulder. "Did you hear what they said?"

He turned around. "Sarah said astronauts on the ISS regularly video chat with their family on earth, but it won't be like that when they go to Mars."

"Oh," I said, relieved that at least one person was talking to me. "Why?"

"Too far away," Thomas said, moving up a bit in the sand. "A message from Mars could take ten or even twenty minutes to get to Earth, and then it would take another ten or twenty minutes to send a message back to Mars. So, you couldn't really have a back and forth conversation that easily."

I imagined what it would be like if I couldn't talk to my mom or dad or Isadora for months and months at a time. Izzy wouldn't even know she had a sister.

"I haven't called my family since that first day," Thomas said, frowning a bit.

In fact, I hadn't talked to my family in a few days either. "We've been so busy, you know?" I said, and my face burned because how was it possible I was too busy to call my own family? I shuffled my feet in the sand, and suddenly felt a wave of panic. What if Izzy's surgery was moved up? I took in a deep breath of the salt air. My parents would call me if that happened, right?

I pushed the thought out of my mind and focused

on Thomas who was taking his turn. "Wow, I can't believe how clear it is. You can totally see all the parts . . . this is so cool. I always thought you couldn't see the ISS through a telescope."

"It's not easy," Marcus said. "You need a telescope programmed to track the movement. With the naked eye, the ISS just looks like a bright star."

I squinted at the sky where the telescope was pointing, and Marcus was right. The ISS looked like a shooting star, bright and moving across the sky. Then my gaze fell upon Ella and Claire, walking by the ocean with their elbows linked like best-friends-forever. How could Ella not see what I saw in Claire? How could she not believe me, her true and actual friend, for one second? Maybe we weren't such good friends after all.

"Okay, Luci, you're up," Sarah said. But when I leaned over the telescope, all I saw was fuzz.

"I can't see anything."

Sarah looked at the sky. "Cloud. Just wait a second for it to get out of the way." She watched as it moved across the sky. "Okay."

But when I looked again, it was too late, the International Space Station was gone, and I was the only one that didn't get to see it through the telescope.

When we got back to the cottage, Claire grabbed the bathroom first, leaving Ella and me alone. We pulled out our pajamas and Ella rubbed lotion onto her dry hands, neither of us talking. For a moment, I thought I saw Ella's face soften and she opened her mouth to say something, but then we heard the toilet flush and Claire was back. Ella took her pajamas into the bathroom and shut the door.

I got dressed and climbed up to my bed, burying myself under the covers. A few minutes later, Claire and Ella were whispering and giggling below me, and once I thought I heard my name.

"What?" I asked.

"We didn't say anything," Claire said.

But I knew they did and I wanted to tell them that I had a rule about friendships and leaving people out of whispering and secrets. It was a rule Raelyn and I made back in third grade and it was definitely our best rule.

They were silent for a minute but then their giggling and whispering started all over again. I couldn't fall asleep, too busy straining to listen, even though I knew I shouldn't. I was afraid I'd hear them talking about me in a not-nice way. Even worse, I was afraid it would be Ella's whisper. And then I'd know we weren't going to be friends anymore and probably I'd never get a postcard from her again. And I wished I didn't care. But I did.

I opened up the window by my bed. Just a crack so I could hear the lapping of the bay and the frogs and the wind instead of Ella and Claire.

The next morning at breakfast, I sat with Dominic, Thomas, and Buzz and we watched the Aviation kids doing calisthenics on the grassy area in their bathing suits instead of their flight suits for a change, getting ready for their day in the pool to practice water survival. I tried to focus on what Buzz was saying about missing bacon, but I was distracted by Claire and Ella eating their breakfasts on a beach blanket under a tree nearby.

When Claire got up for a minute, Ella came over to our picnic table and motioned me toward the big tree. I went, even though I didn't feel like talking to Ella just then. Or maybe ever. I was sweating, and hoped that Ella wouldn't notice, or that she would think it was because of the summer heat.

"I thought a lot about things last night," she said, "and I think if there's any chance of the three of us girls making the dive team, we're going to have to get along."

"Wait," I said. "Does that mean Sarah and Marcus found an open slot for you to retake your test?"

She nodded. "Marcus found an open pool time on Monday. If I pass the treading test, Pirate Pete will take me for a practice pool dive to catch me up to everyone."

"That's great news, Ella," I said. "I'm really happy for you."

"Anyway," she continued. "There's no way Sarah and Marcus will send the three of us to Cetus if we can't even be friends."

I nodded, agreeing with her, but also not really liking her tone of voice. Almost like she was the boss of this situation.

"And I think the only way that could happen," she continued, "is if you apologize to Claire."

"What? No." I took a step away from her. "I was trying to help you. She dropped the stopwatch in the pool and did it on purpose."

"How are you so sure she did it on purpose?" Ella asked.

"Because you were ready for that skills test, Ella.

Like, so ready there was no way you were going to fail. The only reason you didn't pass was because of Claire."

"But don't you think there's a chance she didn't do it on purpose?" Ella said. "Even a tiny chance? You were all fooling around, raising your arms and stuff. It really could have been an accident."

I groaned in frustration, but then stopped myself. I was the one who suggested we do the wave, not Claire. I guess she *could* have gotten caught up in the moment and dropped the stopwatch.

"Luci, we're all on the same team," Ella continued, "and the Cetus mission is no joke. We need to put all of this behind us and put the mission first."

I slumped. I knew she was right. If Sarah and Marcus found out we couldn't get past this, we could say good-bye to our spots on the dive team.

She grabbed my hand. "I don't want to fight with you. I've been looking forward to this camp so we could be together. I'm not asking you to be best friends with Claire. Just don't be enemies."

I sighed. "You should have passed that test, Ella."

"I know," she said. "But stop worrying about me. It stinks that I'll miss the big pool dive, but I'll get one more chance to take the test before Cetus teams are picked. I could still be on the dive team."

I spotted Claire through the windows into the cafeteria. She was coming back.

"Someone once told me that you have to be friends with your roommates," Ella said. "That astronauts have to put their differences aside and get along with their team no matter what."

I smiled, knocking into her with my shoulder. "That is terrible advice," I said, joking, because it was something I had said not too long ago when we weren't getting along all the time at Space Camp.

"Come on," Ella said, whispering now because Claire was marching across the grassy area. "Just apologize. Let's get along. Do it for me. For the mission."

As much as I hated to admit it, Ella was right. If we were on a mission to Mars right now, there'd be no room for arguing or accusing teammates of something—especially if you didn't have proof. All of this could have been in my head. Maybe she *hadn't* moved away from me in the pool. Maybe she *didn't* try to sabotage Ella during her treading test.

Maybe Claire wasn't the problem at all.

Maybe it was me.

CHAPTER 11

FOR THE MISSION

When everyone went to the hangar to get ready for our morning meeting with Marcus and Sarah, I took a quick detour to call my family. I wanted to talk to them about camp and about Ella and about apologizing to Claire. Even though I'd been apologizing to friends for my whole life about little things, this situation felt more complicated. It wasn't like the time I broke Raelyn's charm bracelet, or when I got sticky gum on her favorite bathing suit. This was trickier because it really wasn't clear whether I was the one who needed to apologize. But I knew my parents would tell me to be the bigger person and make things right. They'd know just what to say.

They answered on the second ring, my heart leaping when Isadora's chubby cheeks came into view.

"Hi, Izzy!" I said. She flapped her penguin in the camera. "Hi, Penguin!"

And then Mom and Dad leaned into the

picture, waving as Izzy reached for the sippy cup in Mom's hand.

"How is she doing?" I said. "Any updates?"

"All is well, Luci," Mom said. "Her surgery is still scheduled for the week after you get home from camp."

My breakfast gurgled in my stomach. Did Izzy even know her heart was sick? Did she even know what a big deal this was?

Isadora came back into the picture, almost swinging her cup into the computer before Dad grabbed it, which made Izzy shriek and cry.

"It's okay, Izzy," I said calmly. But she was mad. The red-faced-tantrum kind of mad.

Mom picked her up and shushed her and took her to the window to look at the birds, but it wasn't working.

"How are you doing, Luci?" Dad asked as my little sister screamed in the background.

"Well . . ." I started but Dad was distracted by Izzy trying to fling herself out of Mom's arms.

"It's good?" he asked. "You're meeting friends and having fun?"

All of us worried whenever Izzy had a fit. Worried that it would strain her heart more.

"Maybe I should call back another time," I said.
"I'm doing fine, Dad. Everything is great." I lied.

Dad peered over his shoulder. "Yes, I should go help your mother. We love you, Luciana."

"I love you too," I said, and then we hung up.

I stared at the blank laptop screen for a moment, thinking about how everything was not great and how was I going to fix all of this anyway?

After our morning meeting, I took the long way to the greenhouse, hoping to gather my thoughts before I had to face Claire. I stopped for a minute to watch the Rocket Science kids put the finishing touches on the rockets they'd send off later that day. I took a closer look at the jet engine sitting on a table that the Aviation kids had been putting back together over the week. When I passed the underwater astronaut trainer, Thomas was backing away from a porthole.

"Pretty cool what they're doing in there," he said, walking with me.

"Survival stuff?"

He nodded. "How to live through a plane crash into water."

"Whoa," I said. "That's pretty serious."

He shrugged. "Better to be prepared, though, right?"

We were almost to the greenhouse now and all I could think about was how unprepared I was to talk to Claire.

"Hey," I said, changing the subject. "Have you ever had to apologize for something you didn't really feel sorry for?"

Thomas snorted. "If you're not sorry, why would you apologize?"

I sighed. "Because I want to be the bigger person. You know, for the good of the team and all."

Thomas shook his head. "That's not going to do anything for the team. If you don't mean it, don't apologize."

That was not the advice I was looking for.

"Maybe you're apologizing for the wrong thing?" Thomas said, stopping in front of the greenhouse.

A light bulb flashed in my brain. "Hey, you know, that's pretty genius advice."

Thomas smiled.

"Are you the kid in college?" I asked.

He didn't say anything, but he smiled as he headed to the robotics station.

"Thought so," I called after him.

I stood outside the greenhouse for a second, getting up my nerve to talk to Claire. Ella and Buzz were huddled around their printer, and Dominic and Thomas circled a bin of PVC pipes and robot parts. Thomas was right. I wasn't sorry for accusing Claire of dropping the stopwatch on purpose, because I believed she had actually done it. But maybe I was sorry for the way I shouted it across the pool, the way I accused her in front of everyone. I took a breath, and walked through the plastic flap door of the greenhouse.

Claire looked up from the plant pillow in front of her. She was measuring another seedling. So far we had five sprouts. Sarah had been right; at this rate, we'd be able to harvest a few to send with the dive team to Cetus in a few days.

I sat down on the stool next to her and she stayed focused on her measuring, holding the ruler against the delicate stem of the butter lettuce.

"Claire," I said, the room too quiet except for the hum of the bank of LED lights glowing red and green and blue on the rest of the plants. "I just want to say that I'm sorry. I shouldn't have accused you of cheating in front of everyone like that."

And, truly, I was sorry. If I could do it again, I would have told Sarah or Marcus or Pirate Pete instead of announcing it to the entire room.

She stopped what she was doing, biting her lip and not really looking at me. Would she reject my apology? Make me say it again?

But instead, she said, "Thanks," and went back to her work.

I studied her.

"So, that's it?" I said. "Apology accepted? We're cool?"

She slid off her stool and took the plant pillow back to the grower. "I know you're good friends with Ella, so . . ." She shrugged.

She took another plant pillow and sat down again, measuring each leaf, some of them twice, recording observations into our plant binder with complete focus.

I cleared my throat. "Need help?"

"Nope." She kept working.

"Are you sure?" I said. "I could record while you measure?"

"I'm fine." She rotated her body away from me, pulling her stool in closer to the table.

How could we do the pool dive as partners tomorrow if she was barely even talking to me?

"Claire," I tried again. "I'm sorry that I embarrassed you."

She finally looked up at me. "I know. I heard you. Apology accepted, okay?" And then she went back to her plants.

Usually when someone accepted your apology you hugged or talked about it some more and it was like you were all of a sudden better friends than you'd ever been. Everyone always felt better after a good apology. But not this time. Not with Claire.

It was possible I felt even worse. Like, there was no hope for Claire and me to ever be friends.

I just hoped we could be friends enough to get us through the pool dive tomorrow and, even more important, qualified for the Cetus dive team.

CHAPTER 12

PRACTICE DIVE

The day of our dive to the bottom of the pool had arrived. Claire and I were going to practice our soil sampling EVA for Cetus—as partners, but maybe still not as friends. If we were on a real mission to Mars, we'd be doing a space walk to collect Mars soil and see if we could use it to grow hydroponics in our habitat. But since we were actually going to be in a very deep pool and not millions of miles away on Mars, we'd be collecting ping-pong-sized balls instead, and delivering them to an underwater storage room.

Dominic and Thomas were going to run a set of robo-ops with their underwater robot. Buzz had to stay up top with Ella and Sarah because he still had to take all of his scuba skills tests. Both Buzz and Ella would get one last chance to pass their tests on Monday.

"Once you're at the bottom of the pool, take a few minutes to explore your environment," Marcus said, setting up his own air tanks so he could dive with us. "But then when we turn on the music, that's your signal to begin performing your EVA or robotics operation. From that point on, you'll want to act as you would if you were in space, and complete your task efficiently and quickly."

"That doesn't mean rush," Sarah said, "but don't dillydally either. When you're doing a space walk, you don't want to be outside the spacecraft for longer than necessary."

"Also, this is a partner activity. Rule number one: Stay with your partners at all times," Marcus said. "Scuba diving is a dangerous activity, and so you need to keep your partner within sight in case either of you runs out of air and needs to use an emergency regulator."

We nodded, my stomach all butterflies as I put on my scuba gear.

Claire and I hopped into the pool, and I peered down into the deep blue. I was actually going to scuba dive! I looked at Ella and waved, and for a second I felt sick to my stomach. What if my mask filled up? What if I panicked? In a twenty-five-foot-deep pool, you couldn't just swim to the surface. You had to take your time going up and let the pressure leave your body. It didn't help that I barely even trusted my own partner. I took an extra breath and reminded myself that I was only going to the bottom of the pool, not loading myself into a capsule on top of a rocket headed to Mars. That thought didn't help my nauseated feeling, so I pushed it away and thought of Izzy instead. How many more days until I would see her again?

"You ready?" Claire asked, interrupting my thoughts.

I squared my shoulders, hoping she couldn't hear my heart pounding double-time through my scuba vest. "Yep," I replied. "You ready?"

She nodded.

Pirate Pete swam over to us, suited up in his diving equipment. He checked our gauges, tugged on our air tanks, tightened our straps, and then he gave us the A-OK sign. "Everyone good?" We put our regulators in our mouths and breathed in and out. Pete gave us a thumbs-down. It was time to start our descent.

Pete guided us over to the long ladder, and Claire and I took either side. We went down one rung at a time, taking a break when Claire pointed to her ear, signaling that the pressure was causing her pain. I could feel the pressure too, like the beginning of an ear infection or like how it felt coming out of a loud auditorium. Half hurting and half plugged. We tried swallowing to relieve the pressure in our ears like Pete taught us, and when that didn't work, pinching our noses and blowing out at the same time. Then we continued down a few rungs before stopping again and repeating the process.

I looked up, my ears popping a bit, and I saw the surface: a wavy ceiling so far away. The pool was pretty quiet except for the noises of our scuba equipment tapping against the side of the tank. It was like the entire world was on mute.

When Claire's ears cleared, we continued all the way to the bottom, the weights on our belts just heavy enough to allow us to walk on the floor of the pool, half bouncing, half swimming. Thomas and Dominic were already down there with Marcus, looking out the portholes into the hangar. Buzz must have gone back down the ramp from the pool deck because he was there on the other side of Dominic's porthole, making fish faces and sticking out his tongue.

I picked up one of the bowling balls at the bottom of the pool, surprised that, underwater, it felt as light as a piece of tissue paper. *Is this what a bowling ball would feel like in space?* I wondered. Thomas swam up to me and pointed at a basketball net by the EVA structure. I dove forward, holding the bowling ball over my head, and dunked it like I was a superhero.

Next to the basketball hoop was an even larger ball that looked like it was made of solid concrete. It said "100 lbs" on the side and yet I could pick it up without a problem. Then I tried throwing it to Thomas, which wasn't as easy as I thought it would be. The effort of pushing the ball through the water forced me backward a bit and right into Claire, who was standing behind me.

I touched her shoulder, because I didn't know the hand signals for "sorry, are you okay?" She touched my shoulder back and then motioned to the scuba trainers, who I realized were tapping their watches. Rock music started playing through the underwater speakers. It was time to practice our EVA.

We had already decided before we started the dive that Claire would carry the pail while we collected the samples, and I would deliver the samples to the storage area. I looked over my shoulder at the underwater storage closet. It was past the basketball net and under the giant apparatus made out of PVC piping where the boys were going to test run their robot. I just had to bring the samples into the storage room and leave them there. Simple.

Claire and I swam the perimeter of the pool, filling the pail with the balls, which were so floaty one of us had to lift the lid on the pail while the other one quickly stuffed the ball inside and then snapped the lid closed before they could float back out. The same thing would happen if we were doing our EVA outside the International Space Station in zero gravity. We swam past the boys, Claire grabbing a ball from under Dominic's foot. Thomas handed us another ball that was wedged against one of the pipes. Dominic was running the robotics operation using a waterproof remote control, and the big robot inched forward across the pool floor.

The scuba trainers were perched on top of the PVC pipes, watching us do our jobs. Marcus gave me an A-OK sign and I gave him one back.

Claire and I did one last quick sweep of the pool to look for more balls, and then when we were sure we had gotten them all, I took the pail and swam into the storage area. I spotted the target on the floor at the back of the little room where I was supposed to leave the pail, but when I swam all the way inside, I accidentally hit the door with one of my air tanks and the door slid down behind me.

Startled by the darkness, I dropped the pail, blinking to adjust my eyes. I felt for the door, pushing myself against it, groping for a handle or for any kind of opening. But it was no use.

Not wanting to give up, I pushed and pulled so hard that I felt water seep into the bottom of my scuba mask. But the door still wouldn't budge. I was trapped.

My heart was thumping out of my chest, and I felt as if I couldn't get enough air through my regulator. It was as if I was stuffed into Izzy's little car again with no one to help this time. I banged on the door, but underwater, it made barely any sound at all.

And where was Claire? Didn't she see that the door had shut, that I was trapped? Wasn't rule number one that we were supposed to stay together?

My mind raced. I couldn't scream. I had no voice underwater. I kicked and banged the door, but it was no use. Did anyone else see me go into the storage room? The trainers? Were they watching? What if they all thought I went to the surface without them? How much air did I have left in this scuba tank?

My mask was now halfway filled with water, and panic was creeping up my spine. I reminded myself to breathe through my mouth. Ignore the water in my mask. I was afraid to try and get the water out. Afraid I'd forget how to do it and accidentally get water up my nose. And then what?

My heart was beating so fast and hard, I could hear

it like a drum in my ears and I worried I was having a heart attack. I started feeling dizzy, and I made myself think of the time when Raelyn and I were painting our nails bright blue and Izzy wanted her nails painted too and then she walked around staring at them for the rest of the morning. My heart throbbed.

And then I saw a crack of light from the door. The crack got bigger and bigger until Pete's face appeared and he reached in and grabbed me out of the storage room. He swam me back to the ladder where we went back up, a few rungs at a time. He checked my air gauge and was throwing a thousand hand signals at me, and the only one I could remember to give him was the A-OK sign, even though I wasn't.

Everyone was already at the pool platform when we reached the surface. Even Claire.

She had left me.

Pete guided me to a place on the ledge where I could stand, and Sarah, who had jumped into the water, helped me take off my halfway-filled-up mask and the heavy air tank.

Claire walked over and put her hand on my shoulder, but I pulled away, my heart beating in overdrive again. "You left me down there?"

She looked stung. "I turned around and then all of a sudden you were gone and I thought you went back up already."

"That's a lie," said a voice from behind me. Ella was standing at the side of the pool, a scuba mask pushed on top of her head. "I saw you leave, Claire. As soon as Luci swam into the storage room, you saw Thomas and Dominic going back up the ladder with Marcus and you went with them. If you had stayed with her, you would've seen that she was trapped and could have gotten her out of there sooner. She could have drowned." Her voice was shaking.

Claire shook her head. "Okay, but I was just—"

"Claire," Marcus interrupted. "I thought you were having an emergency. You were giving the hand signal that you needed to go up. That is the only reason I let you come to the surface without your partner. And I had no idea that Luci was stuck in the storage room. I just thought you needed to get up fast and that Luci would follow with Pete."

Marcus seemed filled with guilt, but I knew this was not his fault.

"Claire?" Sarah said, her voice calm and measured. "Were you having an emergency?"

The whole team was around us now, waiting to hear what Claire had to say.

"No, I . . . um . . . I—I didn't know she was stuck in there." Her face was bright red.

"Because you swam away and left her!" Ella said.

"They said no dillydallying!" Claire yelled.

And then there was a shift in the room.

Sarah stepped up to the edge of the pool. "We also instructed you never to leave your partner, Claire. You put Luci in danger because you left. Partners need to trust and count on each other. That is a crucial part of working on a team in space."

Marcus squeezed water out of his bathing suit. "You're lucky that Luci is okay, that something terrible didn't happen. To leave a partner is reckless."

Sarah handed Claire a towel. "I think we need to talk."

Claire took the towel, looking down at her feet the whole time. And then she disappeared down the ramp with Sarah and Marcus.

Everything was silent except for the muffled music coming from the pool speakers. And with no one talking, I had to breathe in and out just to make sure I wasn't still underwater.

CHAPTER 13

TEAM MEETING

We didn't see Claire for the rest of the day. But after dinner, when Ella and I walked to the bay with ice-cream cones, we spotted Claire sitting with Sarah on the front steps of our cabin, her bags beside her in the sand.

Ella looked at me and we steered ourselves away from our cabin to the other side of the beach. We sat on top of a picnic table watching the water, licking our ice cream in silence.

"Luci . . ." Ella started after a few minutes. I already knew what she was going to say. She had been apologizing all day about not believing me about Claire, and I kept telling her to stop because she was my friend, and if you asked me, friends were allowed to make a mistake every so often.

"Really, Ella, it's okay," I said, catching a drip of melting ice cream with my tongue and trying very hard to not look over to our cabin.

"Luci, stop saying that," she said. "It's *not* okay. I should have trusted you. You kept telling me Claire was bad news, and I just kept ignoring you."

"But you had a reason not to believe me," I said, thinking back to Space Camp. "The last time I had a strong feeling about someone, I was wrong, and I got us in big trouble."

She shook her head. "Yeah, sorry for bringing that up so much."

"It's hard, though, when you just have this gut feeling about someone and no real proof, you know?" I said, nibbling on my cone.

"Well, maybe if I hadn't been so wrapped up in being friends with Claire, I would have seen that you were right about the stopwatch and I could have saved you from what happened in the pool."

"That's not your fault," I said.

"I just had this idea of what Lance Jacobs's daughter would be like and how cool it would be to be friends with her," Ella admitted.

"I guess I get that." I finished my ice cream and slid off the picnic table, dipping my sticky hands in the bay.

"I'm sorry for not believing you," Ella said, joining me at the water's edge. "I hope you'll still be my friend."

"Forever and ever," I said. And then Ella gave me a hug, which if you knew Ella was a rare thing.

Our hug was cut short by Marcus, Dominic, Buzz, and Thomas joining us on the beach, Buzz still finishing up his after-dinner ice cream.

"Team meeting," Marcus announced, instructing everyone to sit on the sand. We all plopped down, the six of us forming a circle. I looked for Sarah and Claire at our cabin, but they were gone.

"Is Claire getting expelled from camp?" Buzz asked, crunching into his cone.

"No," Marcus said. "Not expelled. But she has lost the chance to be on the dive team. She'll be in mission control."

"She's *staying*?" Ella said. "Then, why were her bags packed?"

"Well," Marcus said. "Even though she's not expelled, she wants to go home."

"Then she should!" Ella said, and I shushed her.

Marcus gave her a look. "But her father can't pick her up. He's traveling for meetings and can't leave to get her. She asked if she could sleep in the sick bay for the rest of camp, and we are going to let her."

I felt a wave of relief that I wouldn't have to see Claire in the cabin later that night.

"Even in an emergency? Her dad can't come get her?" Thomas said, making a pile of sand.

"What if she broke her leg or fell off the boat and was missing at sea?" Buzz asked. "Would he come get her then?"

Ella groaned. "Isn't there an assistant or nanny or someone who can pick her up?"

My chest ached. If I called my parents and told them I had to come home because it was an emergency, they'd leave that very second to come get me.

Marcus shook his head. "This is not an emergency. This is a youth astronaut training camp and we're all learning here. If we sent every kid home for making a bad decision or a big mistake, we wouldn't be helping anyone. Did you ever make a bad decision?"

Ella and I looked at each other because the answer was yes, but that didn't mean I felt much different about Claire.

"That being said," Marcus continued, looking at me and then at everyone else, "you have every right to be angry with Claire."

And maybe hurt? I mean, how could she just leave me like that? What if we had been in the ocean? I shuddered.

"Claire put a member of her team in danger," Marcus said. "When you're an astronaut, your team is everything. No matter where you are—up in space or training under the water—you need to be able to depend on one another."

Thomas raised his hand. "Can Luci move to our robotic project team?"

Marcus shook his head. "There are only two more days left to work on projects, and we want Luci to stay on the hydroponics team."

"With Claire? Are you serious?" Ella blurted out.

"Yes, with Claire. See, the thing is," Marcus said, "when you're in the real space program, you will not be able to pick your own team. You'll have to work with all sorts of people and some of them will be difficult. You'll need to figure out how to move forward with a project no matter what."

The thought of working side by side with Claire in our little tarped greenhouse did not make me happy. I didn't feel like figuring out how to work with her. Maybe not ever. And why should I?

The next morning at breakfast, we saw Claire with

Marcus and Sarah, sitting in front of an empty plate. Ella made a growly sound, and I stared hard at the ground as we made our way to a picnic table where the boys devoured their pancakes. I did not want any accidental eye contact with Claire because I was afraid she wouldn't even look sorry for what she did.

Buzz put down his pancake. "You probably already figured it out, but I volunteered to be on the mission control team. And it's not because I'm a crybaby scaredy-cat or anything."

Ella blinked at him. "Nobody even said that."

"Maybe you were thinking it."

We all shook our heads.

"Fine. It's what I was thinking." He stared at his hands. "I may be an Olympic swimmer, but I'm just not cut out for scuba diving. I'm much better staying close to the surface. The whole idea of going so far underwater freaks me out and, well, I just don't want to take the chance of ruining the mission or something."

Dominic gave him a half smile. "That's very mature of you."

"Yeah," Buzz said. "So, maybe you should call me Cole from now on since I'm nothing like Buzz Aldrin anymore."

Thomas sat up. "I think maybe you're more like a real astronaut than before."

Dominic nodded. "Sacrificing for the team and stuff."

"Thanks, guys." Buzz's cheeks bloomed a sharp pink, and he returned to his breakfast.

Ella looked to her left and right. "Anyone else want mission control?" But it seemed like the rest of us were still hoping for a spot on Cetus.

"You're going to be okay?" Thomas asked me. "After what happened?"

I thought about it, taking a bite of oatmeal. "Totally," I said finally. But even the *thought* of the storage room made my heart flutter. "Yep, no problems over here," I added.

Because I wasn't about to give up my dream of going to Cetus. Not after I passed all of my skills tests. Not because I had one bad experience in the pool. Not for anything.

CHAPTER 14

THE STORM

We followed Ella up to the pool when it was time for her treading test, and as we passed the greenhouse, I could see Claire's silhouette by the grower. She was working on our project. I had peeked in on our plants earlier that morning when Claire wasn't around. That was my plan for the rest of our time here: to do everything possible to avoid working on our plants at the same time as Claire.

Sarah caught up with Ella and me and she rubbed my back. "How do you feel this morning?"

"Good, thanks," I said automatically, but actually I wasn't completely sure how I felt other than mixed-up. Angry and betrayed and confused, and even a little bit sad and hurt, if feeling all of these things at once was possible.

This time Sarah was in charge of the stopwatch during Ella's treading test, and she wore it safely around her neck. Ella got tired in the last few minutes again, and started to sink a bit. But then Buzz put a pair of fins on his feet and flapped around the pool platform, making everyone laugh, and Ella relaxed. She ended up passing and we cheered and high-fived and gave A-OK signs instead of thumbs-up signs. And then we all watched through one of the portholes as Ella dove to the bottom of the pool with Pirate Pete. They performed the same practice EVA that Claire and I did, collecting balls into a pail and leaving them on the target in the storage area. Except this time, when Ella went into the storage room, Pirate Pete stayed right there and waited for her to safely come out.

Everyone was ready for the next day. The day the Cetus and mission control teams would finally be announced.

When we woke up the next morning, I was almost too nervous about the dive team assignments to eat breakfast. This was what I had come for: to dive to Cetus like so many astronauts before me. Twenty-four hours under the ocean in an astronaut habitat. It wasn't for everyone. But it was certainly the kind of place for a kid who would be the first girl to set foot on Mars.

The breeze across the bay was strong, my ponytail with its purple stripe whipping in the wind. Ella and I paused on the shore to watch the kite boarders and windsurfers scattered in the water, playing in the waves and wind, jumping and flipping high above the bay.

By the time we finished eating in the cafeteria, the wind was fierce and the clouds had turned dark.

"We'd better go," Ella said. "Before the rain starts."

I took one last slurp of orange juice and stood up, my stomach bundled with nerves. When we opened the cafeteria door, it got caught in the wind and I tried catching it, but it slammed against the side of the building.

"Whoa," Ella said. "This looks like a big storm."

The normally calm bay was filled with jagged white waves. We bolted across the grassy area to the airplane hangar, barely making it inside before giant raindrops started falling. Dominic came in right behind us, the door shutting hard against the storm.

He peered out the window. "Look at that!"

Through the window we watched a beach chair flipping down the lawn. The rain picked up fast, turning into a complete and total downpour. It sounded like a waterfall hitting the metal roof of the hangar. And then out of the fog came Buzz, like an Olympic sprinter, racing in so fast that he almost collided with the door when we opened it for him.

He was drenched, a puddle of rainwater spreading around his feet. "Made it," he said, out of breath. His teeth chattered.

We walked over to our meeting table, with a giant view of the storm coming across the bay. Claire was already there, sitting at the end.

Marcus jumped up. "Got caught in the storm, huh?" He ran to get Buzz a towel, and then we all sat down, ready to get our mission roles.

Ella and I crossed our fingers under the table. We wanted to be on the dive team together, of course, but even with Claire being disqualified and Buzz opting out, there was still one kid too many who wanted to go. Dominic, Thomas, Ella, and I looked at one another.

"May the best man get chosen," Dominic said.

"Or woman, thank you very much," I added.

The boys rolled their eyes.

Sarah stood up. "You have all worked hard this week and we're proud of your accomplishments. Ella and Buzz have printed an all-purpose tool on the 3-D printer—"

"And a ton of sporks!" Buzz added.

"Thomas and Dominic have built an effective rover, making changes after running it in the underwater astronaut trainer so that it will be ready for Cetus."

Dominic and Thomas high-fived.

"And from what I've seen," Sarah said, "there are several hydroponic butter lettuce sprouts that Luci and Claire will be ready to harvest tomorrow for the dive team to take onto Cetus."

I glanced at Claire and for a minisecond we made eye contact. Our hydroponics project had turned out to be a success, which was kind of sad when I thought about it since I couldn't say the same about our partnership.

Marcus made a drumroll on the table and through the giant windows behind him, we saw a towel flapping across the grassy area and getting stuck in a gnarled tree branch.

"Reminder," Sarah said, holding up a finger, and Marcus stopped drum rolling. "We are all on the same team. No job is more important than another. We could not do this mission without every single person completing their role."

"Good point, Sarah," Marcus said, returning to his drumroll.

I grabbed Ella's hand. I couldn't help it. My face was

getting hot with the suspense. What if I didn't make it? What if I wasn't good enough? And then my stomach clenched. What if all this hard work—not to mention an almost near-death experience—was for nothing?

"The mission control team will be . . . Dominic, Buzz, and Claire and . . ."

Did that mean—

". . . the dive team will be Luci, Thomas, and Ella."

Ella and I jumped up, squealing and fist-bumping with Thomas. We sat back down when we saw Dominic banging his head against the table in disappointment. We told him it was okay and reminded him that he was still an important member of our team.

But I couldn't believe that I had made it! I was going to Cetus!

When everyone broke to work on their projects, I decided not to start right away and instead snagged the seat in front of the computer and called my parents.

"I made the dive team!" I said when they picked up, leaping out of my chair.

"And me too!" Ella said, leaning into the picture from her spot at the 3-D printer.

Dad clapped and so did Mom, sitting down with a squirmy baby Izzy.

"We're so proud of you, Luci. We knew you could do it!"

It was really happening. I was going to Cetus, the underwater habitat where real astronauts trained before a mission.

And then I noticed something on my little sister's wrist. "Why is Izzy wearing a hospital bracelet?"

She was picking at it, trying to pull it off and shrieking with frustration.

Mom and Dad looked at each other. "We have news, Luci. We just got back from the hospital and Izzy's surgery was rescheduled for tomorrow."

"There was a cancellation, so we jumped on it," Dad added. "It's better not to wait any longer. Everything is going to be fine." He held Izzy's hand for a minute to keep her from tugging on the bracelet.

There was a squeeze in my stomach. "Oh no. Starting tomorrow morning, I'm going to be on Cetus for twenty-four hours. How will I know if she's okay?"

The storm was raging outside now and I peered over my shoulder, hoping Sarah or Marcus wouldn't make me get off the computer in all the thunder and lightning. Ella was there, though, looking at me with a worried expression.

"Luci, you let us worry about Izzy," Mom said. "Your job is to be at camp. Have fun with the other kids and do well on Cetus."

Ella sat down next to me on the bench, hugging me.

"She'll be in surgery for a few hours and as soon as we hear anything, we'll call the camp and leave a message, okay?" Dad said.

"Izzy, where's Penguin?" I said, but she was too distracted, flopping out of Dad's arms. "Izzy?" Did she even know I was here?

"Luci, we have everything handled here at home," Mom said.

"But Mom—" And then with a crash of lightning, the lights flickered and went out, and the entire hangar was thrown into complete darkness.

I was disconnected from my family.

CHAPTER 15

SEA MONSTER

We left for Cetus early in the morning, the sun barely even up, the Aviation and Rocket Science kids still sleeping in their cabins. It was too early to call home one more time. What if Izzy needed me? How would I know if she was okay?

The boat ride to the dive location was bumpy. Ella and Thomas were giddy, trying to get ready while the boat was moving. We needed to wear wet suits in the ocean, so there was a lot of pulling and grunting and getting feet stuck in the wrong places as they struggled to get into their gear.

I decided to wait to put on my suit until we reached calmer waters. Instead, I closed my eyes as we rode out to the dive site, letting the humid air, still a bit cool in the morning, calm me. And it must've worked, because by the time we anchored, I felt a little less worried about things at home, and a lot more excited to be on this mission. I pulled on my wet suit and joined Ella and Thomas in the back of the boat, expecting to see some sign of Cetus under the water. But all I saw was dark ocean.

Sarah and Pirate Pete splashed into the water first. "Ready?" Sarah called up to us. "This is what we've been training for."

Pete gave us the thumbs-down and we climbed in, the water feeling cool even with my wet suit. We descended slowly into the deep green murky water and when we were about halfway down, Cetus came into view. Ella pointed to make sure Thomas and I saw it, but there was no missing the underwater beast.

We followed Sarah around the habitat, which was covered in sea grasses waving in the current, and mussels, oysters, and barnacles stuck to the walls. We swam between Cetus's giant pole-legs dug deep into the sand and then through the complicated pipe structure for EVAs that was bigger and wider than the one in the pool back at camp. I reached out and held one of the pipes. How many astronauts were here before me, performing practice EVAs on this same structure?

There was old equipment on the sandy floor, man-made reefs, homes for crabs and fish and maybe lobsters too. And then we followed Sarah to a platform right under the belly of Cetus. When we stood up, we were surprised to find ourselves in an air pocket.

"Moon pool," Sarah said.

Thomas popped his regulator out of his mouth, looking around. "What . . . I mean . . . how is this possible?"

"Physics." Sarah smiled. "Science is cool."

Pete nodded. "Yup."

I breathed in the salty air that was also a bit stinky, and Ella and I grinned at each other. We walked up a ladder and into the underwater habitat. Someone had already brought our bags and equipment onto Cetus, and we changed out of wet suits into dry clothes behind little curtains.

Thomas finished changing first and we heard him call to us, "Wow, this looks like the real International Space Station. This is so cool! You guys! You've got to see this."

We followed his voice into the next room and stood there for a minute, taking it all in. There was a small table pushed against the wall with booth seats next to a porthole window looking out to the sea. The walls were lined with gauges and dials and cabinets in all different sizes. There was a small sink, an even smaller refrigerator, and a computer station with a microphone to communicate with mission control. Ella disappeared into the other room for a minute and rushed back with a handful of sporks that she had 3-D-printed with Buzz. "Where should I put these?"

"Take some time to look around," Pete said. "Find where everything is and where things go. This would be a good time for you to set up your projects."

The hydroponic garden was in the back of the habitat by the bunkhouse, where there were three triple-stacked bunk beds set into the wall. Mini bunk beds. Practically the smallest, skinniest beds I had ever seen. "Do you guys fit on those?" I said to the counselors.

Pete and Sarah laughed. "Barely."

I pulled my butter lettuce seeds and harvested plants from the cool box, gathered my supplies and brought everything over to a bench. Then, just like Claire and I did on land, I planted the seeds into four plant pillows. I added 100 mL of water to each, set them in the garden tray, and turned on the UV lights. Red and blue and green washed over the white walls.

"Cool," Thomas said, passing me as he brought his

bag to one of the beds. Each bed had its own curtain for privacy. "Have a preference?"

I smiled. It felt nice to get a choice of bunk beds this time. "Nope," I replied.

After Ella finished setting up the kitchen with her 3-D-printed utensils, Sarah and Marcus told us it was time for EVAs. Thomas rolled out of his bed holding the logbook, where all the astronauts and other visitors had written messages and notes about their time on board Cetus.

He pointed to the open book in his lap. "This guy said there's a friendly stingray they named Monty that likes to sleep on the top of Cetus," Thomas said, pointing to the log entry. "They said he'll swim right up to you when you're working."

"Do stingrays have teeth?" I asked, not sure I wanted to swim with a stingray, friendly or not.

"Of course they do," Ella said. "They're related to sharks." And then she saw the look on my face, and added, "But, I mean, they're really small."

Going back into the water meant getting dressed back into our wet suits, which was challenging since they were still wet. I almost punched myself in the face trying to push my elbow into the right place. And Ella's suit got stuck below her knee, and Sarah had to help her tug it up. By the time we were dressed, Ella and I were both sweaty and disgruntled.

As soon as we dropped into the moon pool, though, our feelings of discomfort melted away. It was time to get to work.

"You ready?" I asked, feeling a bit nervous because the last time I did this EVA was in the pool and, well, we all knew what happened then.

Ella nodded, putting her mask in place and expelling leftover water from her regulator.

"Ready, partner," she said.

And, like scuba diving experts, we swam out into the ocean with our sampling containers. We started under Cetus, at the manmade reef constructed from old concrete blocks, where an eel slid out of a hole and nearly scared us half to death. But, being the professional astronaut-scuba-divers we were, we didn't even get any water in our masks.

I took the first set of samples, uncapping my plastic test tubes and sliding them along the ocean floor one by one, filling each with sand before re-capping them.

Ella took the second set of samples by the EVA structure. The entire time, I kept one eye peeled for Monty, the so-called friendly stingray, but except for a few fish and the surprise-attack eel, we didn't see many ocean creatures. But also I made sure always to keep Ella in sight. She was my partner, after all.

If I could have talked underwater, I would have told Ella that I hoped someday we'd be partners on a real space walk, but I couldn't so I gave her an A-OK sign and she gave me one back.

Thomas's robot buzzed by as we were getting our last samples by one of Cetus's giant leg posts. He was running his robo-ops with his remote control from inside the habitat, watching through the porthole by the table, just like he was operating the robot arm on the International Space Station.

When we finished, Ella and I signaled a thumbs-up at the same time and kicked back to the moon pool with our samples. I felt proud of myself. My nerves had been for nothing. And maybe when I got back inside Sarah and Pete would tell me that mission control had a message for me from my parents, and that the message was "everything is okay."

When we got back inside, we peeled out of our suits and changed into our dry clothes once again. Then we joined everyone at the table where Thomas was still running his rover.

"Congratulations on a successful EVA," Sarah told us. "You did an amazing job."

We smiled and Ella and I hugged, accidentally bumping heads. But even with all the good feelings of a job well done, my mind was moving from Cetus, back to Earth, or at least to the shore, and to Izzy.

"Did you hear from my parents?" I asked the counselors. "Is there any news about Izzy?" Everyone was on high alert for me after I told them about Isadora and her moved-up surgery.

"Not yet," Pete said.

"Sorry, Luci." Ella patted me on the back.

"Good news is Sarah is halfway finished making dinner," Pete said, rubbing his stomach. "You guys are in for a treat—we're having real space food. The kind astronauts actually eat on the International Space Station."

"That's so cool!" said Ella.

I nodded. "So, what are we having?" I asked, licking my lips.

Pete grinned, "We'll begin with a fine appetizer of rehydrated shrimp cocktail—"

Ella and I looked at each other dubiously and wrinkled our noses.

"—served on a bed of fresh butter lettuce thanks to our hydroponics experts," Pete continued, bowing in front of me, "followed by Chicken Fiesta, and a sweet dessert of fruit cobbler. Served hot for your enjoyment."

"Is Chicken Fiesta like chicken surprise where you're really not sure if it's chicken or not?" Ella asked. "And that's the surprise?"

Sarah laughed. "Nope. Chicken Fiesta is actually quite tasty. It's flavorful and pretty spicy."

"It has to be," Pirate Pete added. "Being in space can affect an astronaut's taste buds. So, they're always asking for more spices."

"Done!" Thomas announced, holding up his remote control. "I'm bringing our rover in."

Sarah and Pete clapped. "Good job on a successful robotics operation. That's two-for-two for Team Cetus."

Through the porthole, I could see the little robot zooming around the ocean floor, tipping this way and that with the water current.

"Did it get darker out there?" I asked.

Ella looked at her watch. "It's around sunset, so, probably yes, right?"

"Yep," Pete said. "When the sun goes down, it gets darker in the ocean too. At night, when you climb into your bunks and look out the porthole windows, it will feel like you're one hundred feet under instead of thirty."

I shuddered. That was not the kind of feeling I wanted. I looked around. "And you're sure the storm didn't damage our air supply, right?" I was starting to feel a little sick. Maybe we were low on air and didn't even know it. And then we'd all just pass out and—

"Air gauge." Pirate Pete tapped a meter on the wall. "Full, see?"

And then everyone looked at me for a second and I hoped they didn't see that I was sweating a little bit and maybe my heart was beating dangerously fast for a healthy twelve-year-old and—

"It's going to be a while longer till dinner's ready," said Pirate Pete. "Want to ride the bike first, Luci?"

"What?" I wiped my forehead.

He pointed to the exercise bike that he was unfolding in the bunk area. "Everyone has to ride for five minutes," he explained. "If we were on a real ISS mission, you'd have to ride for two hours and forty-five minutes to keep your muscle mass. And if we were on Mars, NASA thinks it would be even longer."

"Oh. Sure," I said. "I can ride first, I guess."

I pulled my damp hair into a ponytail and walked back to the bunk area to get my sneakers out of my bag. But I couldn't shake the feeling that we were trapped down here. I took deep breaths, trying to calm down. I could swim back to the boat if it got to be too much. Right?

Everyone was busy. Ella was helping Pirate Pete set the table, and Sarah was working with Thomas to pull in his robot from the moon pool. They all looked so calm, as if being inside a little tin can at the bottom of an ocean with all this water on top of us was no big deal.

"Maybe we can ask mission control if they heard from my family?" I said.

Pete looked up from putting napkins on the table. "We'll try when you get off the bike. They're taking their dinner break right now. Pizza in mission control. One of the perks of staying on land."

Ella held up a packet of shrimp that were suctioned to the plastic wrapper. "Who needs pizza when you can eat these?"

I managed a smile and started pedaling, hoping to

get this over with as soon as possible so that we could call up to mission control. The bike was loud in the small space, and it didn't do anything to distract me from the growing panic in my gut. What if there was an emergency and I couldn't get out of here in time?

Thomas came in from the wet room, holding up his robot, and Pete slid the trap door to the moon pool closed, latching it tight. Nothing was coming in and nothing was going out.

I pedaled faster.

What if the door rusted shut overnight or the water above us crushed Cetus like a soda can? My heart was loud and thumping hard, making my skin feel tingly and my brain foggy. Was I having a heart attack?

Feeling sick, I got off the bike, and stumbled to the table.

"Are you okay?" Pete asked, helping me sit down. But I couldn't catch my breath, and my heart seemed to be beating faster and faster every second. Was I going to suffocate down here?

"Heart attack," I said breathlessly.

"Does your chest hurt?" Sarah asked, and I shook my head. "Are you asthmatic?"

I shook my head again then tried putting my head between my knees, but there wasn't enough room and there wasn't enough air, and I tried pacing but Sarah and Pete made me sit back down.

I heard Marcus in mission control speaking through the computer speakers. Did he hear from my family?

My heart. Too fast. I heard them talking about medical emergencies and that was exactly what I was having. An emergency. Or were they talking about Izzy?

And I knew one thing: I had to get out of Cetus.

CHAPTER 16

PUSHED TO THE LIMIT

Sarah kept telling me I wasn't going to die, that I would be okay, that I just needed to get my breathing under control before we could swim to the surface.

"Count with me," she said. "Concentrate on breathing in and out. Slowly. One . . . two . . ."

But it wasn't working, and I was still suffocating, my heart racing, and how long until it just gave out?

And then through the computer speaker, I heard a voice. "Luci? This is Claire from mission control."

The last person I wanted to hear from. My face flushed with heat knowing that the rest of the Cetus team was watching my emergency crisis streaming on the giant computer monitors in mission control.

"Believe me, I know exactly what you're going through," Claire said.

I saw Ella cross her arms on the other side of the table and I knew she was thinking the same thing as I was: How could Claire know what I was going through?

"Your heart is beating double time," Claire continued. "You can't catch your breath and you feel like you're going to die, right?"

I nodded, though, because Claire was mostly right. Except I also felt an incredible urge to fling myself into the moon pool and paddle myself to the surface to get out of this place.

Sarah brought the microphone from the communications desk to the table.

"I know what that feels like and you're going to be okay," Claire said.

Or not, I thought, because it wasn't impossible for a kid to have a heart attack every once in a while, and Claire wasn't the expert on everything.

"Look around you. Tell me the first thing you see," Claire said.

I coughed, sucking in air, feeling a flutter of panic run up my back. What if there wasn't enough oxygen for all of us on Cetus? What if—

Sarah pushed the microphone to me. "Go on," she urged. "What's the first thing you see?"

"This microphone," I said.

"What else?" Claire said through the speakers.

"A table, I guess," I said.

"What can you hear?" she asked.

My heartbeat was the loudest thing, pounding in my ears, but I wasn't about to tell Claire that. I listened. "Like, a whirring sound." Probably the refrigerator or maybe the air conditioner.

"Reach out and touch the thing closest to you," Claire said. "What does it feel like?"

I touched the wall. "A little bit cold and hard." This was ridiculous. A wave of nerves hit me again and I tried standing up, but Sarah made me sit back down.

"What can you smell?" Claire went on.

I sniffed impatiently. "Damp things. Like, moisture."

And then Claire started over from the beginning with the same questions until basically I had described the entire kitchen area with every imaginable detail.

Around the third time she asked me what I could smell, I took a long sniff through my nose and realized all at once that I could breathe a little bit better and my heart didn't sound so loud.

"Uh . . ." I breathed in again. "Dinner, I think. Like a spicy, soupy, kind of smell." My face was cooling a bit. "In fact, it's pretty stinky in here."

Everyone laughed, even mission control.

As much as I didn't want to admit it, Claire's trick worked and even after she stopped asking me questions, I went through the exercise again in my head. Sarah rubbed my back and even though my heartbeat had slowed to an almost normal rate and I didn't feel like I was drowning as much, I was still left with an overall sick kind of feeling. Like when you know you failed a test or you forgot your homework at home or you figured out your dreams of being an astronaut were over.

"I think you're feeling a bit better, right?" Sarah said to me. Ella reached over the table and squeezed my hand.

"Can I leave now?" I said quietly, blocking the microphone with my hand so only Sarah could hear. But I saw Ella react to my question, looking at Thomas.

I'd never get to try the shrimp suctioned to its package. I'd never get to sign the logbook. But none of that mattered. Because what were the chances that a girl who couldn't handle a few hours in an underwater habitat would be able to handle an eighteen-month mission to Mars anyway?

If I had proven anything at this camp, it was that Luciana Vega didn't have what it takes to be an astronaut after all.

Sarah looked at me sadly. "Mission control," she said into the microphone. "Please prepare the boat to retrieve a Cetus team member."

"Roger," Marcus said.

Sarah put her hand on my shoulder. "Take a little time to decide whether this is what you really want," she said, getting up from the table.

Suddenly, tears were pouring out of my eyes and I couldn't stop them. Once again I felt like I could die but this time of humiliation for blubbering like a baby. It was like I had no control over anything anymore.

Ella slid into the seat next to me, and Thomas ducked under the table and came out on my other side, both of them squeezing me into a hug, which only made me cry harder.

"Don't cry, Luci," Ella whispered, leaning her head on my shoulder. "You're probably still getting over what happened in the pool."

"That's all I need," I said. "To be claustrophobic or something." Because I was pretty sure if you were claustrophobic, you could kiss a career as an astronaut good-bye.

"Nah," Thomas said. "As Buzz would say, you had a 'freak-out.' That's all."

Pete was back at the counter, taking over dinner,

rehydrating our shrimp packets and Chicken Fiesta sur-
prises. "For the record, I don't know a single astronaut
who hasn't felt scared or out of control at one point in his
or her training," he said.

That was not what I expected him to say.

"Astronauts are always pushing themselves to the
limit," Pete continued. "And they know that things will
get tough and scary but they want it bad enough, so they
work hard and brave through it."

He made it sound so easy to just "brave through it,"
but what if you actually felt like you might die? I never
wanted to feel that way again.

"Getting water in my scuba mask still scares me,"
Thomas said. "A lot."

"Yeah," Ella said. "I don't like that either." She
looked at me, her cheeks turning pink as if she was making a horrible confession. "And if you want to know the
truth, I'm a little bit scared of heights."

I turned to Ella. "I didn't think you were scared of
anything."

"I hate high diving boards and don't even get me
started on Ferris wheels," she said. "And when we got to
the top of the pool that first time, I kind of freaked out.
Even though I acted all brave on the outside."

Pete smiled at us, delivering five packets of shrimp cocktail and plates of butter lettuce leaves to the center of the table.

"And sometimes you might encounter a fear you never knew you had, like sleeping in a habitat thirty feet below the ocean's surface." He nudged me, offering a packet of shrimp first.

I hesitated. I didn't earn this rite of passage. I didn't deserve to eat what real astronauts eat.

"Stay, Luci," Ella said, patting my hand. "We'll all be down here together."

"And if you feel scared again, we can help you," Thomas said.

But even just considering it made me feel a little nauseous and my heart ramped up automatically. I touched the table. Cool. Hard. Smooth.

Just then we heard Marcus's voice on the laptop speakers. "Cetus crew, the boat is ready for retrieval."

Sarah came back into the room and picked up the microphone. "Thank you, Marcus. Please stand by." She turned to me. "Luci, they're ready for us at the docks. Just say the word, and they'll come get us."

I wanted to stay and help my team finish this mission. I really did, but what if I panicked again?

I thought about what Pirate Pete said about how all astronauts felt out of control or scared at one point in their training. Ella and Thomas didn't let their fears stop them from passing their skills tests and making their dives to Cetus. I guess when it came down to it, we were all a little bit scared. If I wanted to be an astronaut, if I wanted to go to Mars, I'd have to get used to being afraid. After all, like Sarah said on the beach that first night, dreams aren't meant to come easy.

"Maybe I'll stay a bit longer," I said.

Sarah raised her eyebrows. "Maybe? Where's the Luciana Vega I met at check-in?"

I smiled. "She's still here." Wasn't she? And would the old Luciana leave her teammates in the middle of a mission? "And she's staying. Definitely."

Ella and Thomas squeezed me into a hug as Sarah told Marcus that the boat wouldn't be needed.

I heard cheers from my teammates all the way back on land in mission control.

I had "braved through" the scariest moment of my life. It was one small step for the Cetus team, and one giant leap for Luciana Vega.

CHAPTER 17

LUCUMA MERINGUE CAKE

I t might not be pizza," Thomas said, all five of us tucked in around the little Cetus table. "But the Chicken Fiesta is not bad."

"And these are the best lettuce leaves I've ever tasted," Pete said, popping one into his mouth. "Good job, Luciana!"

"Has anybody had one of these?" Ella asked, inspecting the orange-ish shrimp on her fork. "It's slippery." She frowned and sniffed. "And smells a little fishy."

Sarah laughed. "First person to down a shrimp gets their fruit cobbler dessert à la mode."

Thomas looked up from his plate. "You have ice cream down here?"

Pete nodded. "The dehydrated kind, which in my opinion is the best kind."

"Let's each eat a shrimp at the same time," I said. I wrapped mine in a lettuce leaf.

"And share the ice cream," Ella added.

And then together Ella, Thomas, and I gulped down a shrimp and it wasn't nearly as disgusting as we imagined. In fact, it was even tasty. And it was totally worth a cube of astronaut ice cream on top of our fruit cobblers.

We were cleaning up the kitchen after our meal when a voice from mission control called to us through the laptop speakers.

"Team Cetus, this is Buzz from mission control. We have a message from the front desk for Luci."

My heart stopped and I nearly dropped the plate I'd been washing into the sink.

Sarah waved me over to the microphone. "This is Luci," I said, my mouth dry.

"I've been asked to pass a message along to you from Earth," he said, and I knew he was trying to be funny about the Earth part, but I was in no mood for jokes.

"Buzz. What's the message?" I urged impatiently.

"I don't get it, but it says, 'Hope you're ready for some lucuma meringue cake when you get home. Love you. Enjoy your underwater adventure.' Oh, wait the last part has an exclamation point so it's more like, 'Enjoy your underwater adventure!'" he yelled.

I grinned. Lucuma cake was for celebrating in our

family. It was our favorite and my mom had my abuelita's recipe from Chile.

"What does the message mean?" Thomas said, Ella standing next to me.

"It means Izzy's okay!" And for the second time that evening, I heard cheers from all around.

Later that night when we got ready to climb into our bunks, Ella and Thomas let me have the bed that had its own porthole looking straight out into the deep. It was strange not seeing the stars at night and not hearing the lapping of the bay right outside the window, but it helped me to be able to look out the window whenever I felt a tingle of worry in my chest or a flutter of panic. It also helped to think of Izzy, recovering from surgery, safe in a bed. And, although I may never admit it to Claire, the thing that helped the most was the trick she taught me over the speaker from mission control.

Before I fell asleep, I thought about Claire and I wondered where she learned her trick and why she would ever want to teach it to me. I was practically her enemy, wasn't I? After all, I was down here and she wasn't.

And then I wondered if she felt like some of this was her fault. That the reason I had this freak-out was because of what she did in the pool. And I thought how maybe she'd be right about that.

But then I realized that I was still down here because Claire had found a way to help me calm down. If it wasn't for her, I wouldn't be sleeping across from Ella here on Cetus—I'd be all alone in our bunk house, wishing things had turned out differently.

But that didn't mean I wasn't the first one into my wet suit in the morning and the first to open the hatch to the moon pool.

"Someone's ready to get back to land," Pete said with a chuckle.

Ella and Thomas took one last look at the habitat before joining me at the door.

Just as I started descending the ladder to the moon pool, Sarah appeared overhead. "Wait! You forgot something."

"I did?" I was supposed to leave all my plant stuff on Cetus, and otherwise the few clothes I brought on board were already packed into the dry bags ready to go.

She waved me out of the moon pool and when I climbed back into Cetus, I saw she was holding the log-book. "Everyone signs."

"Even me?" I said.

"What do you mean, even you?" She poked me in the arm with a pen. "If anyone on board deserves the honor of signing the book, it's you."

I felt my face get warm.

"Just because astronauts are brave does not mean they are without fear. I hope you always remember that," she said. "I'm proud of you, Luci."

She handed me the book. I felt a tingle up my spine as I flipped through the pages, each one covered with names and missions from the past. I blinked tears out of my eyes.

Thomas and Ella had already signed their names:

Ella Emerick, Fail Smart recipient

Thomas Dowdy, College kid

So, I signed my name big and in my very best handwriting:

Luciana Vega, Future First Girl to Mars

When we got back to shore, I dragged Ella with me to the hangar, beelining it for the video-chat station. My heart was thumping hard again because I wanted my parents to answer the phone so bad.

And they did.

"Mom!" I said. "How is she? Is she awake?"

"Luci! How was your night on Cetus?"

"Mom. How is Izzy doing?" I insisted, Ella scooching closer to me on the bench and waving to my parents.

"She is doing as great as we'd hoped." Mom was so close to the screen, and I wished she could pull me right through to the other side. "She's sleeping right now, and they think the surgery went well."

Dad appeared in the screen. "The hard part will be to keep her in bed these next few days." He smiled. "Oh, good morning, Ella. It's so nice to see you." He waved to her, moving his body just enough for me to get a glimpse of Isadora behind them. She was in a crib, with monitors and tubes all around, and her penguin sitting up in the corner near her feet.

Ella grabbed my hand, because if I was being honest, seeing Isadora like that, all still and full of tubes, was a little scary.

"When will she wake up?" I asked. "How long will she have all those things attached to her?"

Mom and Dad looked over their shoulder at her. "Not too long, sweetheart. Those are for monitoring, and she also has an IV to keep her hydrated."

"She's still groggy from the anesthesia and is taking

long naps. But we expect that to wear off soon enough," Dad said.

Ella smiled at me. "Just in time for you to see her when you get home."

"Two more days," I said. "I can't wait."

In a way, I couldn't believe I was still here after what happened on Cetus. Just twelve hours ago, all I wanted was to get out of that habitat, call my parents, and tell them to come get me. I looked at Ella and I knew that if it wasn't for her and Thomas—and even Claire—I probably would have.

"So, tell us about Cetus. Was it amazing?" Dad said.

But then the doctor walked in to check on Izzy and after we blew a thousand kisses to one another and they promised they'd call if there were any updates, we had to hang up.

I turned to Ella. "Phew." There was so much to tell my parents. How I got trapped in a storage room twenty feet underwater. How I thought I was dying of a heart attack on Cetus. How I thought my dream of being an astronaut was over.

All of those stories could wait because in that moment, tired and drained from a successful mission to Cetus, I felt like anything was possible again.

CHAPTER 18

CLAIRE

Ella went back to the cabin to change and shower and take a break. And even though we had omelets for breakfast on Cetus, the rehydrated kind with cheese and little bits of ham in it, I was famished.

I went to the cafeteria, grabbed a snack, and brought it out to the bay, dragging a chair up to the sand and waited for our morning meeting with Sarah and Marcus.

When I glanced to my right, I saw Claire sitting there, looking at the horses on the island across the water. She looked up and for a moment we made eye contact, but then I pretended I was super interested in the chunks of strawberry in my yogurt until she looked away again. I knew I should thank her for helping me last night, but I couldn't get myself to say anything.

I sat in my chair. I ate my yogurt. I tried to enjoy the warm breeze off the bay, but my brain wouldn't let me. I could still see a little bit of Claire without turning my face. I could hear her voice in my head from the night before, calmly telling me how to work through my panic and fear. She may have been the reason why I had a freak-out in the first place because of what happened in the pool, but I couldn't ignore that she was also the reason I was able to brave through it.

So, when I stood up to throw away my yogurt container, I headed for the trash can on the other side of the beach by Claire instead of the one by the hangar. She sat up when she saw me coming, and I knew there was no turning back now, even as much as I wanted to bolt after tossing my yogurt container in the trash can. I had to be the bigger person.

"Hey," I said. "I just wanted to say thank you for helping me last night." I dug my feet into the sand, which was still cold and damp from an overnight shower.

"Don't thank me," Claire said. She snorted. "Not after what I did in the pool."

It was the last thing I wanted to talk about. "It's okay."

"No, it's not," she said.

I watched a snail sliding in the sand. "Yeah. I know."

"Can you sit for a minute?" she said. "I mean, I understand if you don't want to but . . ."

Facing the water, I sat in the sand, but put some distance between us.

"I know it won't mean much, but I'm sorry I left you in the pool." She sniffed. "Like, really sorry." She shook her head. "I got carried away by everything and . . ."

She paused like she wanted me to fill in the blank, but I didn't.

". . . messed things up big time," she said finally.

We were quiet for a minute and I wished the rest of the team would show up already so I didn't have to sit in awkward silence with Claire. I thought about how she could have ruined my entire dream of being an astronaut. What if I always panicked in small spaces from now on? Then what?

I spoke up, angry all of a sudden. "Anyway, what did you think was going to happen when you left me down there?"

"I wasn't thinking," she said.

"No," I said. "When you do something on purpose, it means you thought about it. Hasn't your mom ever told you that—"

I stopped. I didn't know about Claire's mom, only that she never talked about her. Maybe she didn't even have one.

"My mom died when I was a baby. It's just me and my dad," she said. "And his assistant, I guess, and the housekeeper and cook, and I had a nanny until I was ten."

I didn't have a cook or a housekeeper or an assistant, but I did have a family who loved me, and a baby sister with a fixed-up heart, and a best friend—two actually, if I counted Raelyn *and* Ella—and that was worth more than anything.

"Sorry," I said, quietly. "I didn't know."

"It's how it's always been," she said with a shrug. "Just me and my dad. And I got really excited when he said he'd come and do the dive to Cetus with me. He barely has time to do anything with me these days and I . . ." She drifted off, looking at the water instead of me now. "I let things get out of control. I mean, everyone knows I'm competitive. It's not my best quality." She buried her feet deeper into the sand. "But the thought of having to call my dad to tell him not to come because I didn't make the dive team . . . that just wasn't an option for me."

I fanned my face, the sun starting to feel too hot, imagining then what it must have felt like to call her dad to tell him she got disqualified from the dive team. "Did you have to tell him what happened?"

She nodded.

"What did he say?"

She sighed. "Nothing."

If I did something like that to one of my teammates, my parents would have gone on and on and on and then insisted on talking to the camp counselor and then also grounded me for eternity. "Nothing at all?" I asked.

"Yeah, it's what he always does when I get in trouble," she explained. "It's like he's so disappointed in me, he doesn't even have any words. I wish he would just yell at me, though, because when he's mad sometimes it feels like he might never talk to me again."

A silent house. Before Izzy, when my parents had to work late, sometimes it was just me at home and the silence was what I hated the most. That would probably be the worst punishment for me too.

"How'd you know how to do that calming-down trick yesterday?" I asked, changing the subject.

She smiled at me. "I'm scared of flying. And since it's how my dad likes getting around, I had to learn some things about not freaking out."

I laughed. I didn't mean to, it just came out. "Between me being afraid of small places, Ella nervous about heights, and you scared of flying, we'd make quite the space team."

I felt better when Claire laughed too. "You're right. Not exactly the greatest fears to have if you want to be an astronaut."

"But we can work through them," I said, because if I had realized anything through the Cetus ordeal, it's that everybody was afraid of something.

"Well, I'm going to find a way to make all of this up to you someday," she said, getting up, because Buzz and the rest of the boys were coming across the grassy area now, ready for the morning meeting. "If you ever need or want anything, call me, okay?"

"Sure," I said, hoping she really meant it.

We saw Ella bounce down our cottage steps, the meeting about to start in the hangar. When she saw Claire, she stopped mid-stride.

"Ella?" Claire said. She popped up, and I followed as she ran to her even though Ella looked super intimidating with her arms crossed and her face all pinched. It was clear that she was still mad at Claire, and sometimes when Ella was mad you never knew what she was going to say.

"I'm really sorry about messing up your timer," Claire said as we both finally caught up to her.

"I just want to know one thing," Ella said after a second. "Did you do it on purpose?"

And I crossed my fingers, hoping that Claire wouldn't lie to Ella or make up an excuse. That she'd tell the truth even if it meant fessing up to something so mean. Sometimes it was the difference between the whole truth and a little lie that could make or break a friendship for good.

"Yeah," Claire said. "I purposely threw the stopwatch in the water. And I'm sorry."

"Oh," Ella said, looking surprised. "I . . . I just can't believe you'd do that to me. When we were friends."

"I can't either." Claire looked down, like she was studying the grass. "I'd understand if you didn't want to be my friend again."

Ella didn't have anything to say, but I could tell by the way she was picking at her nails that she was thinking about it and it was probably something she'd have to think about for a while. And maybe one day after she'd thought about it enough, Claire would get a post-card in the mail.

"Look, guys," Claire said, standing in front of us. "I know it's going to take more than an apology to make all of this better, but I just want you to know that I feel awful about what happened and how I acted. And from the bottom of my heart, I'm sorry."

I stared hard at Claire, not totally sure if I should believe her words. But her face looked calm and honest, and I couldn't see a speck of bragginess or untruthfulness there. So, for the first time, I believed her.

CHAPTER 19

FAREWELL BONFIRE

We spent our second-to-last day at camp cleaning up our project stations. Ella handed out a bunch of scraps she printed off the 3-D printer, and I got a coin-shaped trinket with a slice through one side.

"It could be like a good luck charm or something," Ella said. "See? I have one too."

"Like a friendship charm," I said.

"Yes!" She seemed very pleased. "Exactly like that." She kissed her coin and then left to help Buzz slide a giant trash bag across the floor.

Claire and I took final pictures of the plants we hadn't harvested for Cetus, measuring their shoots once more. I couldn't believe how much our butter lettuce had grown in such a short time and with so little water. It made me think that growing food hydroponically was a great way to have fresh food up in space. Astronauts millions of miles away on Mars could even make their own salads.

With our projects finished and our Cetus mission a success, we used our last day and a half at camp for fun. Pirate Pete let us snorkel in the bay, collect snails and hermit crabs on the shore, and even take the camp paddleboard out when the Rocket Science kids weren't using it as a platform to shoot off rockets in the water. At first Claire stayed on the beach, but eventually she joined us in the water, and I was proud of my teammates because even though she had made a big mistake, nobody could deny that she was still part of our Cetus team.

On Friday night we had our final bonfire on the beach, a camp send-off before the parents came in the morning. The International Space Station would be in view again, and everyone agreed that I'd get the first look through the telescope this time.

The moon was a tiny sliver when Ella, Claire, and I stepped onto the dark beach and looked up at the sky. The stars were glowing so bright, I felt as if I were floating in space. With the beach and ocean the only things to see for miles, it was like being on a different planet and I felt like a tiny speck in a giant universe.

We sat around our bonfire and snacked on roasted marshmallows. Once my eyes adjusted to the dark, I could see the launch pad next door. They were rebuilding now, construction vehicles and scaffolding and giant pieces of metal scattered around the complex.

"When are they going to finish fixing that up?" I said, pointing my marshmallow stick toward the flight facility.

Sarah looked at it over her shoulder. "Pretty soon actually. They've scheduled a launch in the spring."

"They'll be ready by then?" Ella asked.

"Yep," Marcus said. "When it comes to space travel, there's no time to wallow in failure. They pick themselves up and move on."

Just like that? They were ready to move on?

"Aren't they worried it's going to explode in their faces again?" I asked.

"Well, now that they know what went wrong the first time," Sarah said, "they'll do everything they can to avoid it. But they also know that science and space flight are not always certain. There will always be failures."

"And there will always be discoveries," Marcus added.

I thought about my own failure on Cetus and how if I hadn't freaked out, I may have never discovered that Claire's trick really worked when I needed to calm down.

"It's kind of like without failures there would be no dis-coveries," I added.

Marcus reached over Ella to give me a high five. "Exactly."

Buzz stood up. "I discovered something." All eyes turned to him. "I thought I'd love scuba diving because I love swimming so much but it turns out I don't. But it's okay because I got to realize that mission control is pretty cool. In fact, I want to work in mission control when I grow up."

Sarah and Marcus smiled at him. "Did anyone else discover anything?" Sarah asked, sliding her toasted marshmallow between two graham crackers.

Thomas stood up. "I liked building robots."

Dominic popped up next to him. "Me too. And I discovered that I want to build a lot more robots."

Ella stood up. "I realized that I love scuba diving. And that if you feel like you can't do something, it's just because you need more practice. And don't give up and stuff." She sat back down, her face reddening.

I was trying to think of what to say when, to my sur-prise, Claire stood up. "Uh." She bit her nail. "I realized a lot this week, including that I can be a jerk." She laughed, so we did too. "I thought I really wanted to go to Cetus. I thought I wanted to be an astronaut." She looked at me. "But my favorite part of camp was working in the lab with the plants. So, maybe my future is here on Earth instead of in the stars."

She quickly sat back down, and even though not everyone had forgiven her for what happened in the pool, they clapped because out of her failure, she had made a discovery.

When it was my turn, everyone stared, waiting to hear what I had to say. But I had discovered so many things that I didn't even know where to start.

I stood up, holding three fingers up. "I discovered that rehydrated shrimp cocktail isn't as bad as it sounds, that I can sleep on a teeny-tiny bunk bed without falling out, and that stingrays are related to sharks." Everyone laughed and Buzz threw a marshmallow at me, which I professionally deflected into the bonfire.

The truth was, I wanted to keep my real discovery close to my heart: that even after all that had happened, my dream to be the first girl to Mars hadn't changed.

We heard the chime of Sarah's alarm. She stood up and checked her watch. "It's time. The International Space Station is in view. But only for a few minutes."

We lined up at the telescope, me at the front, my team making sure I didn't miss out this time.

"Go ahead, Luci," Sarah said. "Have a look."

At first, all I saw was the black sky. I bent lower, changing my angle on the lens and all at once it came into view. The International Space Station with all of its modules and solar panels that looked like giant wings. It was right there, so close through the telescope it was like I could reach out and touch it. There were real astronauts living there right now. Eating Chicken Fiesta and rubbery little shrimps.

At one point, maybe they were eleven- or twelve-year-old kids looking at the night sky through a telescope just like me, dreaming about going to space. And maybe it was hard at times and sometimes felt impossible, and maybe they had to brave through it more than once, but in the end, they reached high enough for their dream and they made it.

And all that meant that I could make it too.

ABOUT THE AUTHOR

Erin Teagan is the author of *The Friendship Experiment* and worked in science for more than ten years before becoming a writer. She uses many of her experiences from the lab in her books and loves sharing the best and most interesting (and most dangerous and disgusting) parts of science with kids. Erin lives in Virginia with her family, a ninety-pound lapdog, and a bunny that thinks he's a cat. Visit her at www.erinteagan.com.

To write the Luciana series, Erin went to the real Space Camp at the U.S. Space & Rocket Center in Huntsville, Alabama, where she learned about hydroponics, watched kids build their own rockets, performed a soil experiment, and even scuba dived in the underwater astronaut trainer. Although the activities in this book were inspired by Erin's experience at camp, this second book in the Luciana series takes place in a fictional location loosely based on NASA's flight facility on Wallops Island in Virginia. Unlike in the story, children are supervised during activities and at all times at Space Camp.

SPECIAL THANKS

With gratitude to Dr. Deborah Barnhart, CEO, and Pat Ammons, director of communications at the U.S. Space & Rocket Center, for guiding Luciana's journey through the extraordinary world of Space Camp; astronaut Dr. Megan McArthur; Dr. Ellen Stofan, former chief scientist at NASA; Maureen O'Brien, manager of strategic alliances at NASA; and the rest of the NASA Headquarters and Johnson Space Center teams, for their insights and knowledge of space exploration.

REACH
FOR THE STARS
WITH

Luciana

VISIT
americangirl.com to learn more about
Luciana's world!

Parents, request a FREE catalogue at
americangirl.com/catalogue

Sign up at **americangirl.com/email**
to receive the latest news and exclusive offers

Meet Gabriela McBride™

When the city threatens to close her beloved community arts center, Gabriela is determined to find a way to help. Can she harness the power of her words and rally her community to save Liberty Arts?

Meet TENNEY Grant™

Her biggest dream is to share what's in her heart through music. Little does she know, she's about to get the opportunity of a lifetime.